WHAT IF THE DAUGHTER OF MARY, QUEEN OF SCOTS & LORD BOTHWELL HAD SURVIVED?

THE RETURN OF THE SCOTTISH PRINCESS

SUZANNE BYRNE

The Return of the Scottish Princess

By Suzanne Byrne

This book is a work of fiction. I am obsessed with Scottish history and the life and times in which Mary, Queen of Scots lived. I began to write a book about her life, which has been done numerous times. Then I thought, maybe write about her life from a different angle. There was a world of possibilities. Her life in France, married to Francois, the French Dauphine, or her disastrous marriage to Lord Henry Darnley. I finally settled on her last husband James Hepburn, Lord Bothwell and I ended up with this book.

I started to ask myself what if this had happened? There are thousands of 'what if' scenarios. So, taking some notes from history and adding a little bit of my own fantasy and a little science fiction, I have re-written another plausible story of Scottish history.

It begins with the imprisonment of Mary, Queen of Scots at Loch Leven Castle in 1567. After a short marriage to Lord Bothwell, Queen Mary was captured, imprisoned and forced to abdicate in favour of her son, James, with her half-brother James Stuart (also spelt Stewart), acting as regent. As history records have noted, Queen Mary gave birth to twins while at Loch Leven, Lord Bothwell was their father. History notes do state that the twins were premature and died at birth and were buried on the island on which the castle stood but no evidence of the burial has ever been recovered. Did the twins die? Did one live and taken away for a safer life? What if someone from the future rescued one of the twins and took the baby to the twenty-first century, to a hospital where they could take care of a premature baby.

Then, I thought, what if the baby grew up and returned to Scotland in the 16th century and challenged both her brother, King James VI of Scotland and Queen Elizabeth of England, so that she could rule Scotland herself. There are so many what ifs. My imagination ran away with me.

Much of this story is based on facts.

Queen Elizabeth I did imprison Mary Queen of Scots, and she did have her executed at Fotheringhay Castle. Mary's son, King James VI, did rule Scotland until Queen Elizabeth died without leaving any heirs and left the kingdoms of England, Ireland and Scotland to James, who then became King James I of England, Ireland and Scotland.

Historical facts and dates are accurate, for the most part, except when some events were made up to fit into the story.

There are other places, events and persons of interest, some are mentioned, others not. This story is a work of fiction, it is a story that opens-up a realm of possibilities. If only...If truth be told, with the obsession I have for Mary Queen of Scots, and Scotland, it is my own made up history that I secretly wish I had been part of.

What can I say? History was written, but if time travel did ever exist, it probably would be re-written. With the increasing uncertainty surrounding Great Britain's desire to exit the European Union, it has somewhat ignited a strong fervour for Scotland to gain its own independence.

The English and the Scots have always been at odds, even before King James I tried to bring them together under one rule.

I hope you enjoy a realm of possibilities and the 'what ifs'? Perhaps in another time, or dimension, there is another plausibility, or another historical timeline.

CHAPTER ONE

Dublin Ireland, 2018

Mary Elizabeth rubbed her eyes. She had spent most of the day working on her new historical website. She had lots of ideas, but somehow the site has ended up as a reference site for all things Scottish. It had been a year since she was in Edinburgh and could not wait to get back over.

She remembered the feeling that hit her when she arrived at Holyrood Palace, walking through the same halls that Mary Queen of Scots had, she could not shake the feeling that someone was watching her, but dismissed it as quick.

She sat at her desk and thought of Gran, it would have been nice to make this trip with her, but she was gone, buried a few weeks earlier. Gran had insisted with her last words that Mary Elizabeth make the trip, go do what she had to in Edinburgh but then insisted she make her way to Kinross, sooner rather than later. Gran had not explained the need for urgency, just that it was imperative Mary Elizabeth go to Loch Leven and trace her roots. 'Before its too late,' Gran whispered in her last breaths.

Mary Elizabeth closed-up Gran's house, deciding to extend her stay in Scotland, to follow her grandmother's dying wish. 'Take the ring,' Gran had said, not that Mary Elizabeth would go anywhere without it as it had been on her hand since gran had given it to her on her sixteenth birthday. 'The ring is the connection,' Gran tried explaining, but Mary Elizabeth found her instructions difficult to follow.

Relaxing on the plane, going over every door in Gran's house that she had double locked until her return. It was just her now, she had grown up in that house. Gran was the only parent Mary Elizabeth had ever known. Her parents had died tragically in a car accident when Mary Elizabeth was just a baby. At least that was the story Gran had told her. The two of them shared an inseparable bond right from the very beginning, a bond that only death could break.

With no other relatives, Mary Elizabeth inherited the entire estate, but with funeral costs and the expense of a large house in an expensive city like Dublin, she wondered how Gran ever managed it. What would she do with the house and all of Gran's treasures was a decision she would make when she returned.

Gran had been full of stories about Scotland. She was a great storyteller, but there were times when Mary Elizabeth wondered how much was true. There was one story that had always captured her attention, the one that was bringing her to Kinross, a tiny community about an hour away from Edinburgh. Situated on the shores of one of Scotland's illustrious lochs. Loch Leven, Kinross had a vibrant history that dated back centuries and was famous for the imprisonment of one of the country's most flamboyant monarchs, Queen Mary.

CHAPTER TWO

KINROSS, 2018

After spending two days in her favourite Scottish city, Edinburgh, Mary Elizabeth had arrived in Kinross to fulfil Gran's final wish.

'Is there anything left of the castle?' Mary Elizabeth turned to the young boy, standing beside the waters of Loch Leven. It was bitterly cold.

The boy looked at Mary Elizabeth with bored eyes, like someone who had seen countless tourists wanting to know all the gory details of the fated castle on the island in the middle of the loch. 'Aye,' he said with his thick Scottish accent. 'Not much left just a few stones and crumbled walls. There is the tower, though. Queen Mary was imprisoned in the tower.' Strange how that survived and nothing else did.'

'Is it worth going across the water to visit?' She had to know. Apparently, her heritage was there, somewhere, and she wanted to know if the stories her grandmother had told her were true. It all began on this loch, in that castle. But she did not know the entire story. Gran had insisted that she come to Kinross, to Loch Leven Castle, to study her past and discover the rest of the story for herself.

The boy shrugged his shoulders. ‘Not always bad, try again tomorrow. The storm will pass by then.’

Alone, she gazed out across the rough waters. A storm was brewing, and it was moving in fast. She should find her way back to Mrs. Murphy’s Bed and Breakfast where she had checked in earlier. Her feet seemed anchored to the spot, her eyes were glued on something she could not see in the distance. What was pulling her to this place? The voices whispered inside her head at night, voices that were in English, French and sometimes in Gaelic. She understood these voices, but why were they speaking to her? And what were the blurry visions that were in her dreams, even more so since her grandmother had died? The voices had gotten louder since she arrived in Kinross. There had to be something in Gran’s stories. She had to find out.

As the wind picked up, it blew her deep red curls over her face, Mary Elizabeth’s eyes looked down at her hands. She stretched out the left hand and stared at the ring that was on her baby finger. At the time when Gran gave her this heirloom, she also shared the story of the ring, at least as much as she was willing to share. The ring had been in the family for generations and only the firstborn daughter of the firstborn daughter (and so on) could wear it. The ring was her connection to a past she was not even sure she believed in, a past that had been shared from one generation to the next. Or was there more? Was there more to the story that her grandmother never managed to share?

What was she going to find in Loch Leven Castle? The clues had to be there. But the young boy said it was mostly ruins, except for the tower. Queen Mary’s tower. What could she possibly find to collaborate Gran’s story?

A glow emanated from the ring on her hand and she felt a warmth spread up her arms. The wind picked up, tossing her hair in every direction. She turned and faced the wind, allowing its impact to draw her forward. She took a step, then another, until she felt the waves of the loch splash over her feet. The water was so cold that it jolted her back into reality. What the hell was she doing walking into the loch? What was that strong force pulling her forward?

'Miss.' She heard a voice from behind her as the power continued to pull her into the loch. 'Miss!' A hand then grabbed her arm and pulled her back to the shore. The hands tightened around her as she tried to pull away and return to the loch. Then, she heard a high-pitched scream in the air. She did not know where the scream had come from. It sounded like it came from across the water. It also sounded like it came from within herself.

Another scream and everything went black.

CHAPTER THREE

LOCH LEVEN CASTLE, 1567

'Lord, grant me mercy. Teach me to know that my love for him is pure tenderness and constant.'

'No! No! It cannot be!'

'But it is!'

'Mary. Mary. Mary. Mary. All my Mary's. Come here.'

'Oui Madam.'

'Non, non.'

Screams.

'Poussez! Poussez!'

Silence.

'I want to hold it. I want to hold my baby.' A whispered voice and a sob. 'why is the other baby dead?'

'It was too early!'

Silence. A voice, almost a whisper, sings softly. It's a lullaby. A suckling sound and the voice continued to sing. The wind washes away the sound of the heavy footsteps that are approaching.

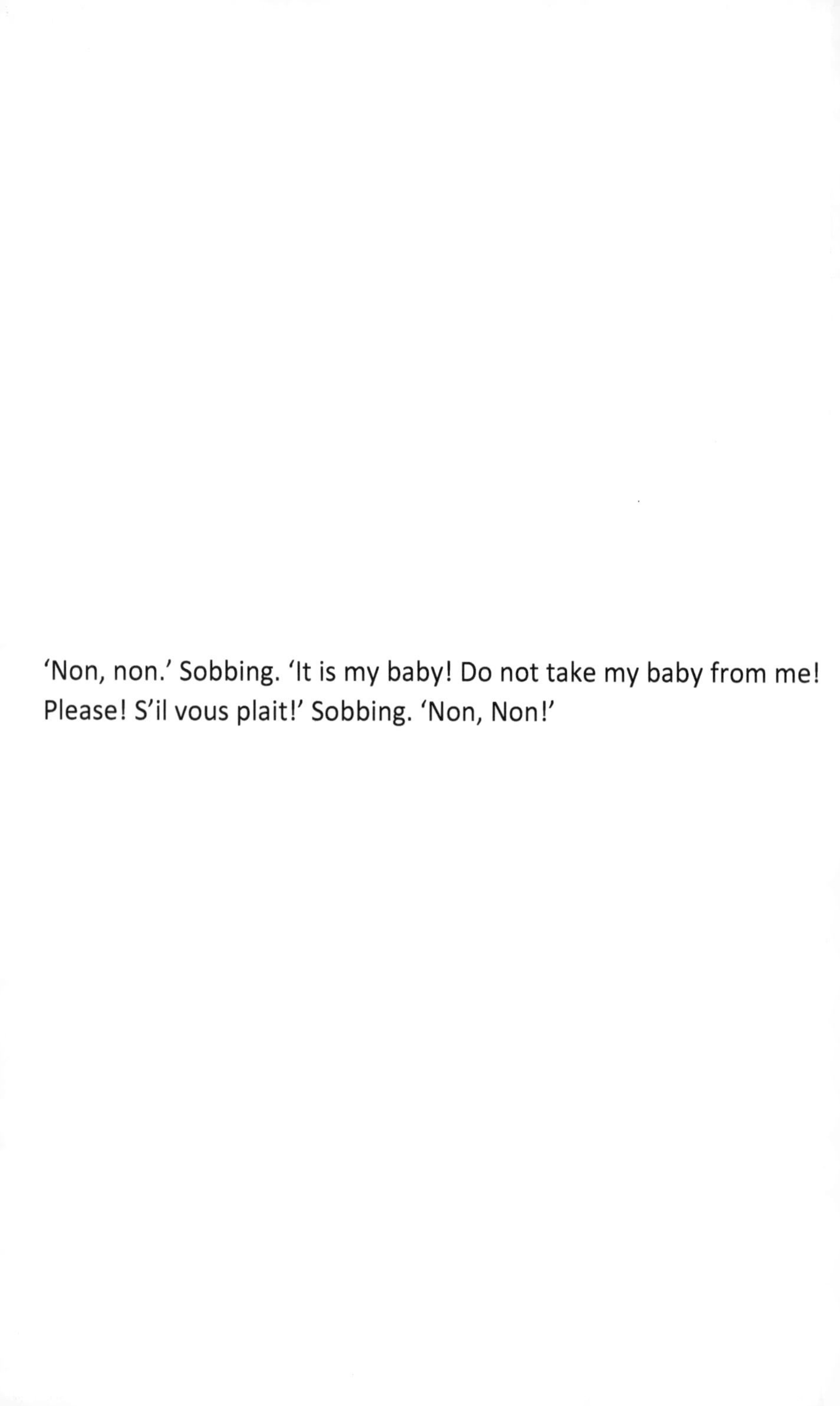

‘Non, non.’ Sobbing. ‘It is my baby! Do not take my baby from me! Please! S’il vous plait!’ Sobbing. ‘Non, Non!’

CHAPTER FOUR

KINROSS, 2018

'Mary Elizabeth Stuart,' a woman's voice cut through the darkness. 'She's Mary Elizabeth Stuart. She rented a room from me for a few weeks. Here. Place her on the couch. 'Get her some tea and I'll see if I can bring her around.'

'I'll be quick, Mrs Murphy,' a man's voice answered.

'No!' Mary Elizabeth screamed. 'Don't let them take my baby!' she grabbed Mrs. Murphy's hand as the woman held a cloth to her head. Mary Elizabeth moved her mouth as she spoke the words, her eyes still closed. 'Don't let them take my baby!'

'What baby?' Mrs Murphy asked. 'Calm yourself, Miss Stuart There is no baby here. No one is taking any baby.'

Mary Elizabeth tried to open her eyes, but they felt like they were glued shut. So many voices rolling around in her head. Which was which? She did not know. Every so often she heard her name, but were they talking about her or talking to her?

'She's coming around.' A man's voice. 'Miss Stuart, can you hear me?'

Mary Elizabeth moaned, turning her head from side to side. Just as quick as the voices in her head had started, they stopped. Her eyes popped open, no longer glued. She tried to sit up. 'Where am I?'

'Lie back. You've had a bit of a spell, my dear.'

'Where am I?' She tried to clear her throat, but it only made her cough.

'At my Bed & Breakfast, dear.'

A second set of eyes were looking at her. Dark eyes that bore into her own, like they were seeking answers that she could not give. Mary Elizabeth couldn't help but shudder and forced herself to look away.

'I don't understand.' Mary Elizabeth said as she slowly pulled herself up into a sitting position. Closing her eyes, she took in a deep breath. She opened her eyes and was relieved that her vision was clearing.

Mrs Murphy leaned into her. 'You were walking down by the pier and were about knee deep in the water and were insistent that you had to walk in further. Then you just blacked out. If Mr Stuart here had not been there, you might have been washed away.'

The stranger from the waterside moved closer. 'James Stuart.' He held out his hand for the introduction. With that thick accent, he was a true Scotsman. 'Another one of the notorious Stuart clan. My friends just call me Jamie. I just arrived this afternoon from Glencoe. After checking in at the best B&B north of Hadrian's Wall. I took a stroll down by the water. It's a good thing I came upon you when I did.'

'I'm fine now, really, thank you. I don't understand what exactly happened out there. I'm here to recover as best I can from the death of a loved one and to research some family history.' Mary Elizabeth relaxed and drank her tea.

She did not want to mention the voices she had heard. Nor did she understand her need to walk into the loch. She looked totally nuts.

'I think some nice warm broth and bread is called for.' Mrs Murphy made her way to the kitchen. 'Come along you two, enough excitement for one evening. Let's have something to eat.'

Jamie held out his hand to help Mary Elizabeth, but she waved it away. 'I'm fine,' she insisted.

CHAPTER FIVE

Mary Elizabeth rolled over, stretching her legs the length of the bed. The duvet covered her like a cocoon. She forced her eyes open but was reluctant to leave the safeness of her room.

The events of the previous day flashed back at her. Her sleep had been deep and unmarred by dreams, which was a blessing. After her ordeal down by the water, Mary Elizabeth was starting to think that she was possessed. And if she was, by what?

A knock on the door made her jump. 'I've brought you some tea and toast.' It was Mrs Murphy.

She opened the door with a faint smile. 'That is so nice of you Mrs. Murphy, but you don't have to wait on me.'

'I just wanted to be sure that you were ok. Don't forget to eat your toast, you need something in you to keep you going.'

'Yes, Mrs Murphy. Thank you.'

Mrs Murphy nodded her head. 'Take it easy today. The weather is a lot better. If you feel up to it, you could go for a walk around the town.'

When Mrs Murphy left, Mary Elizabeth poured herself some tea and sat by the window.

Situated on a rise in the landscape, Mrs Murphy's B&B overlooked the tiny town of Kinross. It was a great view. Mary Elizabeth gazed over the rooftops and down towards the waters of the loch. Her eyes travelled across the waters as if they were being pulled by a magnet, to the island in the middle of the loch. Today the visibility was very clear. She could even see the ruins of Loch Leven Castle. She gasped, startled by the draw she felt toward the island. What the hell was that?

Mary Elizabeth shook her head, forcing her eyes to look toward the opposite end of the loch. As she calmed down, she noticed movement in the woods along the shoreline. The shadow of a rider on horseback came out from the trees, then just as quick, disappeared. Another trick of the eye? Mary Elizabeth wasn't sure, but she was starting to feel more than a little uneasy about what was happening to her.

Looking away from the window, she let her eyes rest on the picture that was hanging over her bed. It looked like an old etching, a black and white image. The image was a castle surrounded by water. Maybe it was Loch Leven Castle, she thought. She would ask Mrs Murphy.

Maybe today would be a good day to visit the island, as the weather looked brighter. She started to study the picture again, it certainly wasn't the castle as it is now. She knew that it was mostly ruins. She had read up about the castle before her trip, wanting to know all the history. The Douglas family had owned the island castle for about 300 years before Mary Queen of Scots was imprisoned there in 1567. Her gaoler, William Douglas, was a harsh man and did not allow the queen many privileges, keeping her under close guard. Early in her imprisonment, Queen Mary had given birth to twins. According to historical documents, the twins died at birth and were supposedly buried somewhere on the island. No trace of the burial has ever been found.

After she finished her tea and toast, she felt ready for the day ahead and dressed. She would take her hostess's advice and walk around the town of Kinross.

Mary Elizabeth made her way to the kitchen with her breakfast tray. 'You didn't need to bring that down.' Mrs Murphy said taking the tray. 'I was coming down anyway.' Mary Elizabeth said getting herself ready.

'Are you off for a walk?'

'I think so, some fresh air will do me good.'

Footsteps could be heard coming down the stairs. Just as Mary Elizabeth was about to turn and make her way outside, Jamie entered the kitchen. 'Ah! I see you're up and about. Off for a walk?

'Yes.'

'Do you want some company?' he asked.

'I was just about to take in the town myself.'

Mary Elizabeth nodded. It wouldn't hurt to have someone nearby in case anything else strange happened. 'Sure, why not. Mr. Stuart, isn't it?'

'I prefer Jamie, Miss Stuart,' he answered with a twinkle in his eye.

'And I prefer Mary Elizabeth.' They both held each other's gaze as if sizing each other up. After a few moments, Mary Elizabeth broke the silence. 'I just thought I would walk around the village and get some fresh air.'

'My thoughts exactly.' Jamie motioned towards the door. 'We can walk together, or I can follow you around like a besotted puppy.'

Mary Elizabeth just laughed.

'We could go over to the island, if you like,' Jamie suggested as he motioned Mary Elizabeth to lead the way. 'Nothing like a couple of Stuarts, maybe even distant cousins, visiting the ruins of one of our ancestors.

'Let's do it.' Mary Elizabeth headed down the hill towards the boats.

'What's your interest in this area?' Mary Elizabeth broke the silence. 'Do you have family or are you just playing tourist?'

'You could say a bit of both,' Jamie answered. 'Though the family thing is ancient history. How about you?'

'Likewise,' Mary Elizabeth agreed. 'My grandmother told me to come. So, I came.'

'Why?'

'To learn things, I guess. I don't know. I suppose I'll find out, or not at some point.' Changing the subject, she asked, 'So what about you, what do you do? I mean, when you are not travelling all over the countryside rescuing ladies who faint on a stormy night?'

Jamie chuckled. 'I work. How about you?'

'Aren't we vague! I work too.'

'Ok. Let's talk about something else. Why Kinross?'

Mary Elizabeth shrugged. 'I have yet to find out.'

They arrived at the docks and found the tour boat, named Mary's Spirit loading passengers for the trip to the island. Jamie helped Mary Elizabeth aboard and they took their seat at the back. As they approached the castle, they saw the remnants of what once was, a grand estate.

Mary Elizabeth had been watching as the boat approached the island castle. She was excited at the prospect of finally stepping foot on the land where Queen Mary had once been imprisoned. She did not understand the pull she started to feel, but she knew she had to visit this place. Not hearing Jamie's last comment, she pulled her eyes away from the island to look at him. 'What?'

He caught her eye. 'Well, you know that we have been fighting for independence for some time. We suffered a defeat in a referendum that will keep us locked with England until the next battle. England has done us no favours over the centuries. I sometimes wonder what would have happened if King James VI had never left Scotland to take over the rule of the two countries from his London throne.

With a lift from her eyebrows, Mary Elizabeth noted, 'That would have been an interesting alternative to the abuse that England brought on the poor Scottish people over the course of time. Would Scotland have managed to persevere on its own?'

'Oh, I think so.' Jamie nodded. 'I know so. And now we have the Brexit debacle.'

Further conversation was interrupted by the boat slowing down. They were approaching the island's dock. Mary Elizabeth could feel the pull intensify. It was electrifying when she stepped ashore and walked slowly towards the castle.

'Queen Mary's tower,' she whispered as her eyes scanned the one remaining structure that had survived. She picked up her pace, walking around the others who were moving slowly towards the ruins.

'Hey, Mary Elizabeth, wait.' Jamie called out. He started to run up to catch her. The other tourists from the boat stopped to look at the woman who was walking like she was in a trance making her way to the tower.

Mary stopped abruptly when she felt her arm being pulled. She turned around and saw Jamie. 'What are you doing?'

'I should be asking you that,' he replied. 'You walked off like a bloody zombie. What is up with you? First you pass out for no apparent reason, then you start screaming about babies. Now you're marching toward the queen's tower as if a magnet was pulling you to it. What gives?'

Mary Elizabeth shrugged her shoulders. Turning on her heel, she continued to march, this time she seemed to be more aware of her surroundings. 'I don't know what you mean. I just want to see the tower where Queen Mary was imprisoned.'

'So, does everybody else, but they didn't push their way past the others in a race to see who gets there first.'

Mary Elizabeth didn't answer, she just kept on walking. Jamie threw up his hands in despair and walked away. 'Have it your way. The last boat leaves at four. I'll meet you at the docks. If you do not turn up, I won't wait for you.'

'Fine.'

Mary Elizabeth climbed the wooden stairs that led to a doorway halfway up the tower. The stairs were obviously recent. She entered the tower and took a deep breath. It was damp and musty, from years left unattended. Remnants of stone alcoves and benches lined the walls next to the window openings.

This was where the Queen of Scots resided for almost a year. Not at all pleasant. A gust of wind threw Mary Elizabeth off balance. Cries could be heard from above. 'Mary Elizabeth, come quickly,' a woman called from the top of the stone stairs that had now appeared.

Mary Elizabeth studied her surroundings. The walkway on which she had entered was now gone. She was standing on a stone floor, a progression of stairs along the far wall, led upwards. It was very dark. Candles were lighting on the walls. The door behind her was closed tight; the door that had not been there earlier when she entered.

'Mary Elizabeth.' The voice was more insistent. 'Come. The queen needs you. She needs us all. NOW.'

Mary Elizabeth started to climb the stairs. Whatever was happening had happened for a reason, and there was only one way to find out what the reason was.

'My goodness, child,' the woman exclaimed when Mary Elizabeth reached the top of the stairs. 'Where on earth did you find that outfit? Didn't you think to dress appropriately before coming to see your Queen? Here.' She tossed a cloak over Mary Elizabeth's shoulders. 'That should do for now until we can find you something decent to put on. But for now, we must attend to the queen's needs.'

A scream came through the walls and echoed from one stone wall of the square tower to the other.

CHAPTER SIX

Loch Leven Castle, 1567

Mary Elizabeth pulled the cloak tightly around her waist with the sash the older woman had provided. She bit her lip as she scanned the room. 'It'll have to do for now. At least it is night and the lights not so good.'

She pushed Mary Elizabeth further inside. She had not spoken a word since her world toppled, jostling her into this unknown place and time. She was too confused to make any sense of what was happening to her, not to mention what was happening around her.

She noticed a bed against the wall covered in sheets. A figure writhed and moaned and there was blood everywhere, on the sheets, the floor and on the women, who moved quickly around the bed. Another scream pierced the room and Mary Elizabeth had to fight the urge to cover her ears. She wondered if she could try escape. Knowing that she should not be there. She didn't belong.

A squeak broke the silence that followed the last scream. The ladies hovering by the bed spoke in guarded whispers. Mary Elizabeth struggled to make out what they were saying. She took a step closer, feeling the pull, the need to be a part of what was happening. As she approached the bed, she started to recognise what was being said. The women were speaking French, an older version of the French that she had studied at school.

'She lives,' one of the women whispered, looking down at the tiny blob lying in the palm of her hand.

'It's not possible,' another woman said. 'It is too soon. Much too soon.''

'Too soon! Too small too, she will not live long.'

'But it is possible.' The old woman who had beckoned Mary Elizabeth elbowed her way next to the woman holding the whimpering baby. Continuing in French she added, 'Hand her to me. We must keep her warm. Was there another baby?'

The woman holding the baby handed her to the old woman, who quickly wrapped her in a soft, warm cloth. 'Yes. It was blue. No life. A boy.'

The woman in the bed moved. 'Mon bebe.'

The old woman gently placed the tiny, wrapped bundle in the woman's arms. 'Keep her warm, my lady. She is fragile.'

'Will she live?'

'Not here, my lady. The lord gaoler will see to that. We must spirit her away. Tonight. Before anyone knows that she lives.'

'Not yet. I must hold her for a few moments. She is mine. My own precious baby. My precious little princess. Mary Elizabeth. She must be called Mary Elizabeth. Princess Mary Elizabeth.'

The women standing around her exchanged glances. It was obvious from their expressions that no one had expected the baby to live, at least not long.

'Is she here?'

'Yes, my lady.' The old woman beckoned Mary Elizabeth closer.

'Another Mary Elizabeth?' The woman in the bed studied Mary Elizabeth. 'You look so familiar. Do I know you?'

'No, my lady.' Mary Elizabeth adopted the formality of the conversation that she had just overheard. This woman on the bed was obviously someone of great importance.

'Take her.' The woman handed Mary Elizabeth her tiny bundle. 'Keep her safe. Help her live.'

There was no time to respond. As soon as the tiny princess was placed in Mary Elizabeth's arms, the door which she had entered earlier shot open. The figure of a man appeared.

'The baby. Give it to me now.'

Instinctively, Mary Elizabeth backed into the shadows and wrapped her cloak around the tiny baby, who was starting to wiggle gently in her arms. One of the women carried a lifeless bundle to the man.

'It is a boy, my lord,' she said.

'I heard a baby's whimper,' the man shouted.

'The little prince died shortly after he entered the world, my lord. It was just too early.'

'Humm! Take care of it then and clean up this mess.' He turned around about to leave and stopped abruptly. Without looking at anyone he shouted a command. 'I expect you to join us for dinner tomorrow. Make yourself presentable.'

'Her majesty might not be able to join you tomorrow,' the old woman said.

The lord gave her a cold stare. 'She is no longer 'her majesty'. She is merely a guest in my home and she will join us for dinner.'

But my lord...' one of the other ladies tried to speak.

'No but's. Make it happen. This is my home. Not hers. She is nothing now. She is now just another lady of no means.'

'But she is our Queen,' the old lady tried to argue.

The lord spat on the floor. 'She is not my queen. She gave up that right when she made us all a mockery for the world to see. The Earl of Moray is our Regent until young King James is old enough to rule.' With that, he stormed out of the room.

The room fell silent. The old woman pulled at Mary Elizabeth's arm. 'You must leave. NOW.' After looking outside, the room to make sure the coast was clear, the old woman ushered her out of the room. 'There is a boat waiting. We will take the baby, you and I, before it is too late. The baby must live. Go Now. William is at the boat. He knows where to go. I will meet you there.'

'I do not understand.' Mary Elizabeth didn't know what to say. 'What is happening? Who is that awful man and who is that woman on the bed? Who is this baby?' She felt a gentle nudge pointing her towards the stairs.

Even if she did not fully understand, Mary Elizabeth was starting to realise the gravity of the situation. She grabbed her cloak tighter around the tiny bundle. She did not believe that it had a chance to live, not in this time and place, wherever she was. The baby must be at least four months premature, way too young to survive. But she didn't have time to think. She made her way to the island's shore.

'Over here,' a voice called out to her in a whisper.

Mary Elizabeth followed the voice. She could just make out the figure waving at her. As she approached, the figure reached out and helped her climb aboard. She sat on a bench and wrapped the cloak more closely around her. The wind was picking up and threatened to whip it off her shoulders and she knew she had nothing else to help protect the little princess. Then it hit her. She was rescuing a baby princess. The woman in the bed, the woman who had just given birth, had called her Princess Mary Elizabeth.

'We must be off.' The man pushed the boat away from the shore. The shadowy outline of the island castle drifted further away as the dark night seemed to swallow up everything around them. There was just Mary Elizabeth, the man in the boat, who she assumed was William, and the tiny baby.

As a million thoughts raced through Mary Elizabeth's head, the man brought the oars alongside. He stood, then jumped out, landing in the water with a splash. 'Come along.' He reached out his hand to steady Mary Elizabeth as she attempted to step out of the boat.

As she stood by the trees, she heard a horse nearby, then another. Had they been discovered already? Where had William disappeared to? She jumped when a shadow suddenly appeared. It was William. 'Come along, now. Horses are ready. You can ride, can't you?'

'Yes,' Mary Elizabeth spoke her first word.

Mary Elizabeth felt awkward as the man from the boat lifted her into the saddle. Usually, she was quite capable of mounting by herself. But it was not everyday that she had her arms wrapped around a living treasure.

She followed William in silence. The only sound was the horses' hooves. They rode at a casual pace, even with their need to increase the distance between them and the loch's castle.

Finally, William pulled his horse around to face Mary Elizabeth. 'Alva.' William nodded in front of him. 'The Glen is just over the rise of land. You can hear the waterfalls. It's a beautiful sight to behold. One of many lovely vistas in all of Scotland. Its extremely difficult to make a living off this land, but we Scots are a tough people. We survive. We are the MacGregors, loyal to Queen Mary. This is one of our many crofts. The old lady you met at the castle is one of us. She should be here by now. If not, she will join us soon. Time to get that babe near a warm hearth. Does it still breath?'

'I think so,' Mary Elizabeth whispered. Her free hand felt the baby's chest until she found a pulse. 'The heart is beating, but she is weak.'

'The old woman will know what to do.' William did not say anything else before bringing her into the dark cottage. Mary Elizabeth leaned against the doorframe as she entered. It was a traditional Scottish croft dwelling. Mary Elizabeth had read about Scottish crofts. Gran had instructed her to read everything she could find on Scotland and Scottish history. It was her heritage.

She could smell the burning peat in the hearth as she entered. A voice called out in both Gaelic and English, 'Cead mile failte. Welcome.'

'She speaks Gaelic, Aiden.' Mary Elizabeth recognised the voice. It was the old woman. It took Mary Elizabeth a few minutes to catch on to the thick Scottish accent, but it was like music to her ears. She had loved learning the language as a child, and it all came back to her very quickly. Just as well, she thought, as the old woman continued to speak in Gaelic. But how did she know that she could speak it too.

'Ah! You are here at last.' She reached out to welcome her, or perhaps she was just reclaiming the bundle she had left in Mary Elizabeth's care. 'And how fare the baby?'

'She lives.' Mary Elizabeth replied. She slowly unwrapped her shawl, revealing the tiny princess.

'I must take her from here quickly. There is no time. Were you followed?' she asked William.

'I do not believe so.'

The old woman turned to another woman standing at the hearth. 'Fetch that gown and give it to Mary Elizabeth.'

The figure moved towards her with something draped over her arms. 'You must look the part while you are here. What you wear underneath the cloak will not do in this time and place and there is no time. It is only a matter of minutes before they track us to this cottage. I must leave at once to ensure the baby's safety and her survival. You must be dressed appropriately to play your part and play it well.'

'But where will you go? And what is my part?' Mary Elizabeth asked.

'Not now. Another time, another place. You will know when the time is right, my child. For now, you must find your way back. You must go home.'

'My way back?' Mary Elizabeth was now more confused. 'I don't even know for sure, where I am now.'

A clatter of hooves approached the building. Mary Elizabeth studied her surroundings with concern. 'Go change, quickly. Now. Before it is too late.'

Kate moved her into the back room. Mary Elizabeth scanned the room again as the sound of the horses stopped outside the cottage. The old woman was nowhere to be seen.

CHAPTER SEVEN

Alva, Scotland, 1567

'Where did she go?' Mary Elizabeth shook her head in total confusion. 'The baby. She took the baby. Where did she go?'

Mary Elizabeth was not sure what was going on or what had happened to the old lady or the baby, but she knew from the urgency of Kate's voice that she should act, and quickly. 'Put this on.' Kate handed her a long white gown with some sort of plaid design around the edges.

'An Arisaid.' Mary Elizabeth noted as she pulled it over her head.

'Aye. I have heard it called that.'

Kate helped Mary Elizabeth pull it down over her other clothes. The gown draped down to her heels, hiding any evidence of her jeans or sweater. She wrapped a leather band around Mary Elizabeth's waste and fastened it at the front.

'Slip this on.' She handed Mary Elizabeth what looked like some sort of vest. Mary Elizabeth slipped it on over her shoulders and Kate helped fasten it closed with a brooch. 'It is a Stuart brooch,' she explained. 'The old woman gave it to me to pass it on to you. Mind you don't lose it.'

'I will take very good care of it.' Mary Elizabeth whispered.

The two made their way back to the others in the main room. 'Sit.' William said under his breath.

Mary Elizabeth took a seat by the fire next to William. 'What is happening?'

There was not time to explain as the door crashed in, and a storm of armed men arrived.

'Stand and pay homage to your Regent,' one of the soldiers commanded.

William motioned for Mary Elizabeth to rise with him. The others who had yet to introduce themselves stood up. One of the MacGregors went forward and bent to one knee. 'My Lord,' he said. 'Welcome to my humble abode. Come warm yourself by the hearth.'

'And who dares be out on such a night?' the tallest man in the group of soldiers demanded to know. After a few minutes, when no one in the cottage had spoken, he swung round to face them. 'Whose horses are tied outside?'

As the light caught his features, Mary Elizabeth let out a gasp. James Stuart, Earl of Moray, Regent of Scotland. He was recognisable. But was he the same James, aka Jamie Stuart, who had accompanied her to the castle?

The regent studied the source of the gasp. 'You!' He pointed to Mary Elizabeth. 'Who are you? You are not a MacGregor, for certain. You look more like a Stuart, one of us. What are you doing here?

Mary Elizabeth gave a deep curtsy, not sure of the proper etiquette when greeting a Scottish regent in a crofter's cottage. She kept her cloak well wrapped around her.

'My Lord'. Looking up, she couldn't help but adding in a whisper, 'Jamie, is that you?'

'I beg your pardon!' the regent bellowed. 'No one dares call me Jamie.'

'I am sorry, my lord. I tend to stutter when I am nervous.' Mary Elizabeth bowed her head, still holding her pose in a curtsy.

'Oh, rise up woman. I cannot abide a woman who grovels. Who are you? And what is your purpose here?'

'Mary Elizabeth Stuart, my lord.'

'What?' 'Not another Mary, and a Stuart at that. We cannot be related. Are we?' He bent forward to take a closer look. 'You have her look about you. It is uncanny. You could almost pass for her. And that brooch. Where did you get that brooch?'

'I do not know, sir.' Mary Elizabeth took her time to choose her words carefully. She didn't know how to answer about the brooch, so she said, 'Are not all the Stuarts somehow related?'

It was not the right thing to say. James Stuart, Regent of Scotland, was not amused. 'Grab her. She must be a spy or a traitor. Either is punishable by death.' He pointed his finger at the rest of the occupants. 'The rest of you stay here. I will deal with this troublemaker.'

One of her captors mounted his horse and dragged her up behind him. 'Do not try anything foolish. And do not think for a moment that your name will protect you either. If our Lord Regent decides that you are a danger to him or his country, he will dispose of you without a second thought. Look what happened to our former Queen. She crossed swords with too many people and made too many enemies.'

Mary Elizabeth shivered as he spoke. The regent rode several horses in front. He may or may not have heard what his men were whispering about and what they would do to Mary Elizabeth, given the chance, but he must have heard some. 'She is a Stuart,' he growled at his men. 'For better or worse, she is a Stuart and shall be respected even unto death. I will hear no more unseemly plots from my men. If I do, they shall face the same punishment as the lass.'

Mary Elizabeth was not entirely sure where they were headed. They must be returning to the loch. The trek through the woods did not take as long as it did with William earlier. Perhaps they were taking a more direct route. As the night started to lighten, Mary Elizabeth heard the telling sounds of water hitting the shores. The island castle loomed in the distance.

Mary Elizabeth groaned as she was lowered to the ground and then dragged, towards the water and thrown onto a boat. She could hear voices from the island's shore.

'Who goes there?' a voice called out.

'James Stuart, Earl of Moray, Regent of Scotland.'

Once they banked, the men jumped out of the boat, and followed their leader up the steep slope to the castle. Mary Elizabeth was lifted out of the boat and carried as far as dry land. She was then dragged up the hill, not caring that she had stumbled to maintain her balance. While the regent and his men followed the castle guards into the courtyard, Mary Elizabeth's captor yanked her away from the others, and headed straight to the tower. Queen Mary's tower.

They climbed the stairs but did not continue the climb to the queen's chambers. Instead, her captor took out a large ring of keys from a hook on the wall and made his way to the nearest door. Once the lock released, he pulled open the door and pushed Mary Elizabeth inside. She landed against the far wall with a thud.

'It pays to know one's way around a castle,' he sneered. 'I know where you are. Despite the regent's insistence of pride for the Stuart name, I shall make sure to have some fun with you before you meet your maker.' With that parting threat, he slammed the door shut.

'He is a mean one,' a voice whispered from across the cell. She was not alone.

'Are there others?' Mary Elizabeth's voice crackled as she sat up against the stone wall.

'Just me,' the voice replied. It was difficult to determine whether the voice was male or female.

It was far too dark to make out any form, but the voice confirmed Mary Elizabeth's fears. She was locked in a tiny cell, a dungeon. She was so exhausted, she was too weak to care what might happen next. Her eyes closed and she slipped into oblivion.

CHAPTER EIGHT

Kinross, 2018

'Mary Elizabeth.' A little shake on her shoulder startled her. 'Mary Elizabeth, wake up. What are you doing here? And what is this you are wearing?'

Mary Elizabeth forced her eyes to open. 'Where am I?' She pushed herself up, looking around the space where she lay her head against the wall. 'What is this place? Jamie. What are you doing here?' She could feel dampness around her lower legs and reaching down, she noticed that her skirt was soaked through.

Skirt? Now she was confused. She had dressed this morning in jeans and a sweater. What was this gown? And why was she wearing it? Flashes of events popped into her head. There was a tiny baby, a rescue of that baby, a horseback ride through dark woods and a croft in the glen. Alva Glen he said. Gran had often talked about Alva Glen, its beauty. She had shown her pictures of the area. Mary Elizabeth had always wanted to visit the place, but not in the dark and not with a tiny baby to protect. And then they had thrown her in a cell, with someone else, who she couldn't see. Who? Why?

Jamie chuckled. 'We came over together. Don't you remember? We came to see the castle ruins and you wandered off by yourself, all weird-like.'

Mary Elizabeth shook her head and tried to stand. Jamie lent a hand. 'Easy now.' He said. 'You've obviously banged your head. As for your list of questions, I think it was a cell for prisoners at one time.'

Mary Elizabeth looked around her surroundings. It did indeed look like a cell. There were no windows, just the one opening where a door used to be.

'where is she?' a voice called in the distance. It was unmistakably the Regent's voice.

'In here, my lord.' It was the man with the key, the one with the evil look in his eye.

A key clicked in the lock. The door creaked open. 'Where is she?' the voice demanded.

'I swear my lord. I put her in here. Locked her up myself.'

'But there's no one here, is there?'

'No, my lord.'

'Where is she then? Are you going to tell me that she just up and vanished? And was there not another prisoner in here as well? Where is that prisoner?'

'My lord, I cannot explain it. I do not know what has happened to her or the other woman.'

'You know what happens to those who cross me. Where is she?'

'I do not know, my lord.'

'Perhaps a few days in the cell will jog your memory, then.' And the door clanked shut

'No, no!' Mary Elizabeth moaned. She covered her ears in the hope of blocking out the voices. She was trembling from head to foot as she tried to stand.

'Careful,' Jamie held her.

'You have had a bit of a scare. You were out cold a minute ago.'

'You would know.' Mary Elizabeth leaned against the wall for support. The room was spinning. 'You were there. You had me put in this cell.'

'What?' Jamie said. 'What are you talking about?'

She didn't wait for an answer. She kept one hand on the wall for support and made her way to the doorway. 'I have to get out of here. I do not want to go back there. You were planning to have me executed.'

'You're not making any sense, Mary Elizabeth.' Jamie moved to walk beside her. 'But yes, you should get out of here. The last boat will be leaving soon, and I don't think either one of us want to spend the night on the island.'

It was all Mary Elizabeth needed to hear to move herself quicker. She found her way outside the tower and stumbled down the stairs. She fell in step with the other tourists. Safety in numbers. She didn't know what was happening to her, but it was downright scary, and she didn't know whether she could trust Jamie.

She sat as far away from Jamie as she could on the boat. Nothing was making sense to her. Not the castle, not the tower, or the people she had met.

The boat pulled up beside the dock at Kinross. Mary Elizabeth quickly got out and ran up the hill to Mrs Murphy's B&B. She burst through the door shouting for Mrs Murphy.

'In here, child. I'm in the kitchen.'

Mary Elizabeth found her sitting at the table with a cup of tea in front of her. 'Oh my. Have you been to a fancy-dress party in the sixteenth century?'

That was all it took for Mary Elizabeth to break down in a flood of tears. 'I don't know what's going on. It's all a mess. And a confusing mess at that. What's happening to me?'

'Looks like you have been on a bit of an adventure,' Mrs Murphy said. 'I did wonder last night, when that lad Jamie brought you in. And now today you return dressed in period clothing. You've had a bit of an adventure in time, that's what I think.'

Mary Elizabeth looked up and dried her eyes and stared at Mrs. Murphy with pure shock. 'What?'

'Time travel, my love.' Mrs Murphy raised her eyebrows. 'Your Gran travelled through time. Did she not tell you?'

Mary Elizabeth shook her head. 'How did you know my Gran?'

'Oh, she and I had some adventures together, we did.' Mrs. Murphy laughed. 'Mostly in the sixteenth century, but they were grand adventures. Yes, they were. Now it's your turn. And I believe you have a task that you must perform, which is why you are being pulled into specific events and times frames. It is all rather confusing at first, but you'll catch on in no time.'

'And what about this Jamie fella?' Mary Elizabeth asked.

'He was there. He's the regent.'

'Is he now?' Mrs. Murphy raised an eyebrow. 'I think we both need a cuppa and we'll just have to watch what we say and do around Jamie. At least, until we know for sure.'

Just as she said the last few words, the man himself walked in. 'I wondered if you were here already.' How much had he heard?

He didn't waste time covering his expression. Smiling at Mrs Murphy, he said, 'Ah! Just in time for tea, I see.' He pulled out a chair and made himself comfortable. 'She gave me a right scare today. I found her curled up in a corner of what was once a prison cell in the tower. Queen Mary's tower.'

'It is strange, isn't it?' Mrs Murphy agreed, pouring the tea. As their hostess carried the tea pot to the table, Mary Elizabeth sat quietly, fussing with the tartan shawl that still hung over her shoulders.

'It's the Stuart plaid.' Mrs Murphy noted. 'The Royal Stuart plaid, if I'm not mistaken,' Jamie added.

'Yes, I do believe you are right.' Mrs Murphy took her seat. 'I had no idea you planned to go further than the village today and take in the ruins of the island castle. Not that it's any of my business. I hope you didn't overdo it.

'And now she's had another episode,' Jamie added.

Mary Elizabeth glanced up at Mrs Murphy. She knew my Gran. What else don't I know?

CHAPTER NINE

Mary Elizabeth made her way to the kitchen the following morning. She filled the kettle and heard the front door open and close. When she looked up Mrs M arrived with her shopping. As Mrs M moved around the kitchen putting her supplies away, Mary Elizabeth finished making the tea and sat down at the kitchen table, trying to sort out her thoughts on the previous day's adventure.

Mrs. M sat down beside her. 'You've had a tiring couple of days, my dear.'

'Yes, I have. Tell me, how many of us are there? Who are they? And how will I know which of them are good or bad?

'Oh my, So many questions. Well, I do not know. No one knows who they all are.'

'But you must know some of the time travellers.'

'Aye, lass. I do. You catch on as you meet them in this time and in other times. You just have-to play along, like you do with everything else in life. But more importantly, you need to find out what the purpose is for you in this time travelling exercise. I know you don't fully know your place, yet, you will.

'Mary Elizabeth was intrigued. 'How well did you know my Gran? You said she was a time traveller, too? She never told me.'

'I cannot answer all of your questions,' Mrs M said. 'But, yes, I knew your Gran very well. She and I were the best of friends in this time and in other times. I miss her, but I know I will see her again in another time and another place. That's one of the benefits of time travel. Everything is relevant to time and place, even to life and death. Its like a continuous series of events, none of which is perceptibly different from the others, but each event ultimately affects another event. The important thing to remember is that whatever you do in the past will inevitably effect the time line in the present.'

Mary Elizabeth listened to her every word. 'There have been a lot of movies and books about time travel. I have watched and read a few. Fascinating, but I never believed it was possible.'

'Oh, its possible. And happens all the time.'

Mary Elizabeth sat quietly for a few minutes, pondering the concept of time travel. 'is there a purpose to all this?' Why does this happen? And what are we, or more specifically, what am I supposed to do when I'm tossed back into the sixteenth century? And what do I do about Jamie, if he is a time traveller?

'I understand that you have a lot of questions.' Mrs M took her time to sip her tea. 'I don't pretend to know or understand it all. And I certainly don't have all the answers you are looking for. As for Jamie? If he is a time traveller as you suspect, and he is the regent who oversaw the throne of James VI after Queen Mary's imprisonment, then he may be someone to keep a close eye on. Maybe he might be trying to change some of the events that led to his assassination in 1570.'

'1570! That's only a few years after Mary was imprisoned and forced to abdicate.'

'Yes, it was, so perhaps he does have some sort of agenda. Did he say anything significant to you on your boat ride over to the castle?'

'Not really. Just that he was involved in fighting for Scotland's independence and that this Brexit scenario is making Scottish people more determined to separate from England.'

'Well, then.' Mrs M nodded. 'Perhaps his agenda has something to do with preventing Scotland's initial amalgamation with England when King James took the English crown after Queen Elizabeth died. The tension between England and Scotland has been building over the centuries.'

'So, what is my purpose in all this?' Mary Elizabeth had to ask. 'Why send me back in time? All I did was rescue a premature baby and take her to a safe house. I think it was one of the twins born to Queen Mary. Didn't she give birth to twins while she was imprisoned in Loch Leven Castle?'

'Yes, she did.' Mrs. M studied the younger woman intently. 'You witnessed the birth?' Mary Elizabeth nodded. 'Its written in the history books that the twins were born too early and had died at birth. Their bodies were supposedly buried on the grounds, but no one has ever found their remains.'

'The babies were quite premature,' Mary Elizabeth admitted. 'But what I witnessed and assisted in was the rescue of the twin girl. The boy did not survive. The Lord of the castle, oh no, what was his name?'

'Sir William Douglas.'

'Yes, that's him. He came into the chamber and demanded to know about the birth. The ladies only told him about the boy, that he was dead. He ordered them to dispose of the body, but no one mentioned the girl.'

'Then how did history books record the birth of twins?' Mrs. M questioned.'

'Someone must've recorded it, perhaps someone told the regent.' Mary Elizabeth suggested. 'After all, he did confront me at one of the MacGregor's croft and had me dragged back to Loch Leven and imprisoned me there. So perhaps he knew, but by then the living baby girl was long gone. The old lady took her. Where, I don't know. She just seemed to vanish.'

'The old lady?'

'Everyone seemed to call her that. She never gave me her name.'

'Mary Catherine,' Mrs. M informed her. 'Her name was Mary Catherine. Did you recognise her?'

'I thought, I did, especially since she seemed to know who I was and why I was there.' Mary Elizabeth said. 'Another Mary. Queen Mary surrounded herself with Mary's. And she even named the wee baby Mary Elizabeth. Odd that the little Princess was given my name, don't you think? And how was it that the old lady seemed to expect me on the night the babies were born?'

'So many questions.' Mrs. M pushed back her chair. 'I'll make us a fresh pot of tea. As for the rest of your questions, I'm afraid you will have to find out for yourself. You need to go home, to your Gran's house, and do some looking around. I'm sure you will find your answers there. I know she kept a journal.'

'She did?'

'Hello!' Jamie's voice came from the hall. 'Anyone here?'

'In the kitchen.' Mrs. M shot Mary Elizabeth a warning look. 'We'll talk later.'

'Did I hear something about tea?'

Jamie asked as he entered the kitchen. How long had he been listening? If he heard Mrs. M mention tea, then he had also heard her mention Gran's journal, and perhaps more.

CHAPTER TEN

Mary Elizabeth knew she should get up and dress. Mrs. M had insisted that she make plans to return to Dublin immediately. The episode at the castle had been too close for comfort-too many evil things had almost come to fruition at her expense. The big question on her mind, who was this Jamie Stuart who had accompanied her to the island? Was he a time traveller and the Regent, Queen Mary's half-brother, in the sixteenth century?

She had so many questions. Would she ever get the answers? She took a deep breath and realised she couldn't hide out in her room all day. First thing after breakfast, she would book a flight. She needed to return to Gran's house. She must find the journal and learn everything she could before she found herself in another time warp unprepared and as confused as ever.

She packed her bags, ready to leave as soon as she booked her flight. She made her way downstairs and into the kitchen.

'Ah. You're up, lass.' Mrs. M greeted Mary Elizabeth with a smile.

'Have you seen Jamie this morning?'

'He left about an hour ago. Checked out, he did. Don't know what that guy's up to, but I think he did hear more than he admitted to yesterday. You need to be very wary. He may show up anywhere. And you need to get back home as soon as possible.'

'Here you go, lass.' Mrs. M placed tea and toast in front of Mary Elizabeth. 'Eat up and then make your calls. You want to get the next flight out. Unless you want to try your luck at time travel and take yourself back to Dublin that way. It would be faster.'

'You mean like 'beam' across the water?' Mary Elizabeth laughed. 'I'm not sure I trust myself to arrive in one piece.'

'I could help you,' Mrs. M suggested. 'It would certainly get you home faster. Time is of the essence, I fear. Especially with that Jamie boy on the loose, wherever he's gone.'

Mrs. M stood up from the table and motioned Mary Elizabeth to follow her. 'Come. Let's do it.'

'First of all, you have to acquaint yourself with the various access points to make the jump. And you just happen to be inside one right now.' She didn't wait for a response, just left the kitchen with the expectation that Mary Elizabeth would follow her. At the bottom of the stairs, she stopped briefly to give the young lady instructions. 'Go change into your sixteenth century clothing and meet me here at the end of the stairs. Only bring what you need.

Mary Elizabeth did as she was told. When she returned downstairs, Mrs. M was waiting. She, too, was dressed in costume much like Mary Elizabeth's. 'Come.' Instead of turning into the parlour where Mary Elizabeth had been laid out that first evening after her fainting episode, Mrs. M opened a door opposite the parlour. Mary Elizabeth followed Mrs. M and was surprised to see how big the space was. It certainly wasn't a closet, more like a study.

Book cases lined the walls and, before Mary Elizabeth could take it all in, Mrs. M reached for one specific book on the far wall and pulled it out. Mrs. M poked her hand behind the book and fidgeted with something. She replaced the book, shifted it to the left and the entire bookcase started to move. 'Come quickly.' She motioned to Mary Elizabeth. 'Stand beside me.'

The room started to fade, and the smell of peat smoke invaded her nostrils. 'Greetings Mary Catherine,' the familiar voice of Callum MacGregor spoke from the fireplace. 'I see you've brought our Mary Elizabeth, but I fear you cannot stay. The Regent is on his way here. Again.'

'Aye! We can't stay,' Mrs. M replied. 'We have places to go and people to see. We shall return, though, and will be ready to make our cause known, even to the Regent himself if need be.'

'What cause?' Mary Elizabeth shot a look between the laird and her hostess. 'And he called you Mary. You're the old lady.'

Mrs. M flashed a guilty smile. 'Yes, I am. But there is no time to explain. Come along now.' Mrs. M led Mary Elizabeth to the back room where she had changed her clothes that fateful night. 'Next stop, your Gran's house in Dublin.' She knocked on the wooden table once, then paused, then knocked another three times, just as a thundering noise erupted outside the front door crashed open, the room dimmed, and Mary Elizabeth was back in Gran's house, in her study. There was Gran working away at her desk as she had always done.

'Gran?' Mary Elizabeth stood abruptly. 'I thought...' She stared at her travelling partner. Mrs. M just shrugged her shoulders.

'We're in Dublin at your Gran's house, but before your trip to Scotland, and before Gran passed away.' Mrs. M gave her a brief explanation.

Mary Elizabeth remembered the day very well. It was several weeks before Gran passed away. They had been sitting in the cosy study, Gran at her desk, Mary Elizabeth on the couch, just like they always did over the years. Gran had been reading an article online about Mary, Queen of Scots, one of their most frequented topics of conversation.

'Historians have always claimed that the twins were buried on the island,' Gran had said. 'But no remains have ever been found. I wonder why.'

'I wondered, too,' Mary Elizabeth said. 'Only now I know.'

'What was that, Mary Elizabeth?' Mrs. M startled the young woman out of her flashback.

'Oh, sorry, I was just recalling the conversation Gran and I had the first time this day happened.' Mary Elizabeth wrinkled her brow, trying to focus.

Gran started to laugh. Oh, Mary Elizabeth had missed her laugh. 'Come give me a hug, child,' she said. 'I have missed you.'

Mary Elizabeth didn't wait. She ran and was in her Gran's arms, hoping this hug would last forever.

'Now.' She studied both ladies. 'What's the meaning of this jump in time?'

'We have an assassin on our trail,' Mrs. M explained. 'At least that is what we think. And, with any luck, we'll avoid the poison this time that killed you, or I should say will kill you in a few days' time. Now, we have a lot of work to do before Jamie finds us.'

'Jamie? You don't mean the regent, the Earl of Moray?' Gran raised an eyebrow. 'He's always been a thorn in my side. I did not realise he was a time traveller, too. That does complicate things.'

'I'm afraid so. And I believe he is on his way here right now. On a mission of his own, or so he will say in his defence.'

Turning to Mary Elizabeth, Gran asked, 'You have the ring?'

Mary Elizabeth held up her hand to show that the ring was firmly on her finger and was safe.

'I see you also have the brooch. Did Callum give it to you?'

Mrs. M answered before Mary Elizabeth had a chance to. 'Kate gave it to her. She helped her dress before the regent invaded the cottage.

'How did you know?' Mary Elizabeth stared at the woman with confusion all over her face.

The older woman just shrugged.

'I think I need some answers now.' Mary Elizabeth said. 'I have to know what's going on.'

'And answers you shall have,' Gran's fondness for her granddaughter was evident in the way she looked at her. 'All in good time.'

'No Gran. I need to know now.'

CHAPTER ELEVEN

DUBLIN 2018

The front door bell shattered the silence. 'Who could that be? I'm not expecting anyone.' Gran asked.

Mrs. M and Mary Elizabeth both shook their heads. No one moved.

'Will I answer it?' Mary Elizabeth asked.

Gran quietly walked to the window and let out a groan. 'It looks like the regent, but I cannot be sure. I haven't seen him in a few years and the last time I did, he was a lot older than he is now.'

'And that was in another century, I believe,' Mrs. M added. 'I was there with you. It was the day of his assassination, wasn't it?'

'Yes, it was. Mere moments before he left Linlithgow only to be gunned down, that was the first recorded assassination with a firearm.' Gran paced the length of the room, from the window to her desk and back. She did her best thinking when she paced.

The doorbell rang again. 'We'll have to answer it.' Gran suddenly stopped. 'It's better to have him where we can see and watch him, rather than have him hiding in the shadows.' Turning to Mary Elizabeth, she instructed. 'Go answer the door. I'm sure he'll be surprised to see you. Though, on second thought, maybe he won't. You never know with the regent.'

Mary Elizabeth nodded. 'We shall follow you and greet him as he enters.'

Mary Elizabeth reached the door, flipped the lock, and opened it. She wasn't sure, but she thought she noticed Jamie flinch when he saw her. He recovered quickly and greeted her with a big smile.

'Mary Elizabeth,' he said, his smile forced and his eyes bulging. 'How nice to see you again, and all dressed up for a costume party. I think you must like your new look.'

Mary Elizabeth forced her own smile in response. 'Come in, Jamie.' She closed the door behind him. Gran and Mrs. M stood waiting at the bottom of the stairs. 'You already know Mrs. Murphy, of course.'

'Yes, of course.' Jamie's look was almost gleeful. 'How good to see you, and so soon.' He lifted an eyebrow and then quickly corrected his expression. 'I see you're dressed for a costume party, too.'

Mrs. M didn't answer. She kept her pose, standing one step behind Mary Elizabeth's grandmother.

'And this is my gran...'

Before Mary Elizabeth could say anymore, he approached the women and met Gran's stoic look with one of his own. 'I know. We've met before. Many times, in many different times, and places.'

'James Stuart.' Gran ducked her head slightly in recognition. 'How good of you to visit me in my home. What brings you to Dublin? Or perhaps I should ask, what brings you to the year 2018?'

Jamie bent his head in acknowledgement of Gran's greeting, then paced around the hall. 'Quaint home.' He stopped to come face with Gran. 'But not quite up to your usual standards, is it?'

Gran lifted her right eyebrow in response. 'Follow me.' She led the way into the sitting room. 'Have a seat, Jamie. We may as well be civilized.'

Shaking his head, Jamie let out a forced chuckle. 'Civilized. Right. Not much civilization in these quarters, is there Marie?' He stood and started pacing the room, taking his time to loom over the others, who remained seated on the couch.

'You have no right to call me by my given name, in this century or in the past,' Gran started. 'Now state your purpose.'

'My purpose has always been the same.' He held Gran's eyes, his gaze never leaving hers. 'Maire,' he added with no trepidation. 'Or should I be addressing you as Your Majesty?'

'What's he talking about, Gran?'

Mary Elizabeth asked, her eyes darting from Gran to Jamie and back again to Gran. 'Why does he call you Marie? And Your Majesty?'

'She doesn't know, does she?' Jamie slapped his side. 'Well I'll be...'

'No swearing in this house,' Gran warned.

'I think you should tell your granddaughter the whole truth,' Jamie went on. 'If you don't, I will.' Gran just stared at him. 'As you wish. Your Gran, as you call her,' Jamie tore his gaze from Gran's and fixed it on Mary Elizabeth, '-is your grandmother, in both the present and in the past, in the sixteenth century. She is Marie de Guise, second wife of King James V of Scotland and mother of Mary Queen of Scots. She was regent during Queen Mary's infancy and died, some say of poison, in 1560. Your mother, my dear Mary Elizabeth, was none other than Mary Queen of Scots, herself. You are the twin who lived. It was Mrs. Murphy, the old lady, as you called her, who brought you to this time and place and saved your life. Because you surely would not have survived another day as a preemie in the sixteenth century.' Turning back to Gran, he arched his eyebrows. 'Did I sum up everything adequately?'

Mary Elizabeth sat stunned for several minutes, then turned to face her grandmother. 'Gran, is it true?' Is all that he has said true?'

'Yes, it's true, my dear little princess.' Jamie smirked. 'I should add, my dear cousin, that we are related, but not quite the way you have surmised. Yes, the resemblance is uncanny, but, then again, the Earl of Moray, James Stuart, your mother's older illegitimate brother, is my blood uncle. I inherited his title. Now, if you haven't already guessed, the real purpose of this little charade involving time travel is to ensure that Scotland never unites with England. And that, my dear Princess Mary Elizabeth, is where you come in.'

'Me?'

'Yes, you.' He paused to let the facts sink in. 'Oh yes! I forgot to add that Mrs. Murphy is one of the many Mary's that surrounded both your mother and your grandmother. She was, and I guess still is, your grandmother's most trusted confidante.'

Mary Elizabeth didn't know how to digest all this information. She had been there, in the past, holding the premature baby girl, Queen Mary's surviving twin. She had helped rescue that baby. Could she have been that baby? Was she the daughter of Mary Queen of Scots? How could she exist as two beings in one-time frame? It was all too much to take in.

'Now look what you've done,' Gran scolded Jamie. She reached her arms around her granddaughter for comfort.

'She has a right to know.' Jamie was defensive.

'Is it all true, Gran?' Mary Elizabeth turned to face her grandmother, tears trickling down her face. 'How could I be there holding myself as a baby? A person can't exist twice in one time and place, can they?'

'Yes, my child.' Gran patted her granddaughter's shoulder. 'It is all true, all that Jamie has told you. I am your real grandmother, I am the mother of Mary, Queen of Scots, who was your mother. You are quite right that one person cannot exist twice in one time, but this was an anomaly because you had just been born and were not quite living yet. And if my dear friend here, who you fondly refer to as Mrs. M, had not taken you from that time and brought you to the present, you would probably not be living then or now. Preemies did not live long in the sixteenth century, if at all. Mrs. Murphy brought the baby, Princess Mary Elizabeth, you, here to Dublin, and I immediately took you to the emergency department at the sick children's hospital in Crumlin, where they placed you in an incubator. They saved your life.'

'But how did you explain it to the authorities?' Mary Elizabeth wiped her eyes.

'It was not easy, my dear child. I made up a story that I heard whimpering outside my back door. When I went out to investigate, I found you wrapped in a blanket. The police and children's services got involved then, but nothing proved me in the wrong. I then applied for custody of you and, by the time the courts approved my application, you were old enough and strong enough for me take you home. Mrs. Murphy stayed here and helped me raise you until you were about two, then she returned to Scotland. That's why you haven't met her before, or, at least you don't remember meeting her. We both remained in this time, believing it was safer until you were old enough to accept your purpose, to be the Queen of Scotland, the Queen that the Scottish people of the sixteenth and seventeenth centuries wanted.'

'Whoa! Hold on a minute!' Mary Elizabeth held up her hands as if in surrender and jumped off the couch. She started to pace the floor, pausing long enough to stand in front of Jamie to give a distinct glare that this was all his fault. 'Even if all of this were true and I am Princess Mary Elizabeth, Queen Mary's daughter, there is the little issue about my brother, who was already King James VI of Scotland and later King James I of England, Ireland and Scotland.'

'But,' Gran held up one hand to stave off argument, 'Since James was in England, the Scots became slaves of English landlords and were treated very harshly and unfairly for generations. All of that history can be avoided if another rightful heir, you...' She gave her point more credence by pushing herself off the couch and standing directly in front of her granddaughter. 'Yes, you, Mary Elizabeth. If you were to take charge and challenge King James I of England, you could legitimately take the throne of Scotland and keep the country a free nation for future generations.'

Jamie then cleared his throat and added, 'Then we wouldn't have this blasted ongoing conflict and demands to separate from England. We could rule our people, our way, and decide for ourselves whether or not we want to remain in the European Union.'

'Do we trust him?' Mary Elizabeth pointed a finger at Jamie while looking at both Mrs. M and Gran.

Mrs. M just shrugged her shoulders.

Gran did not answer right away. 'Choose your friends wisely and keep your enemies close. Always the best of advice. I guess we'll have to trust Jamie for now.'

'For now,' he repeated with a deep chuckle.

CHAPTER TWELVE

Mary Elizabeth continued to pace the floor of the sitting room. Gran had decided to trust Jamie, for now, even insisting that he stay in the guest room. She gazed at the fireplace, they rarely used the fire, there was no need with central heating. Something else she would have to give up if she chose to live in the sixteenth century. That and so much more, electricity, plumbing and the internet!

Did she want to give all that up? Was ruling as Queen of Scotland, five hundred years in the past, her purpose? Changing the time line, and the course of events, may only be a means of postponing the inevitable.

She was finding it hard to accept her grandmother's explanation. She could just about get her head around the idea of living her life in the 16th century, as a princess, maybe even with Jamie at her side. If Jamie was regent, his purpose would be limited since he was assassinated in 1570, years before Mary Elizabeth would resurface in Scotland to challenge her brother and reclaim Scotland's right to remain independent. Everything was so confusing.

She began pacing the floor again. The fact that she had witnessed her own birth, then rescued herself, blew her mind. She made her way to the window to try and calm herself. As she looked out, she noticed several men in black suits making their way quickly up to the house.

'Gran', she called, stepping away from the window. 'Gran', she was screaming now. 'We have company.' She ran into Gran's parlour where Gran and Mrs. M were quietly talking. Locking the door behind her, she turned to face the two women. 'We have company, and they do not look friendly.'

'Time to go.' Mrs. M insisted, pulling Gran along with her. Gran was now dressed in 16th century clothing. Gran ran over to her desk and grabbed something before following her faithful friend. Looking at Mary Elizabeth she said, 'the adventure begins now, my child. I am glad you are still in your traditional clothes. We are all dressed for that time now.'

Gran wore an elegant 16th century robe, one that Mary Elizabeth had never seen before, except in illustrations of women in the Royal Scottish court.

'What about Jamie,' Mary Elizabeth asked.

'No time. He's probably already gone on ahead.' Gran then followed Mrs. M to the bookcase in the corner and motioned Mary Elizabeth to follow. Mrs. M pulled out a biography about Mary, Queen of Scots. Fitting, Mary Elizabeth thought as she watched the wall give way to a narrow space and an even narrower staircase.

Mrs. M pushed Gran and Mary Elizabeth up the stairs first, pulling the doorway/bookcase tightly closed behind them. Just in time as a huge crash indicated that whoever had arrived at the house had just broken in.

'Who are those people?' Mary Elizabeth gasped as she ran up the stairs. 'And where are we going?'

'Somewhere safe, but not in this time,' Gran replied.

'They were probably agents from the English court. Mrs. M said from behind Mary Elizabeth.

'Which court?'

'Your brother's court. He knows you're coming, and he wants to protect his realm. All of it.'

'Not dressed the way they were, they all looked like James Bond in the secret service.' Gran stopped, 'Then we had better get you out of this time. It appears that even the powers that be from 21st century want to prevent you from changing time and keep Scotland free and independent.

They reached the top of the stairs, or so it looked. There was nothing else in front of them, just one final step.

An explosion from below sounded and Mary Elizabeth felt herself hurtling through space. She landed with a heavy thud. She felt the ground wet and she was soaked. Looking around, she tried to take in her surroundings. It was dark and all she could see where shadows.

'Gran', she called out. 'Mrs. M.'

'Over here, child.' She started to crawl her way over in the direction of Gran's voice. It was bitter cold, and the ground felt icy.

'Where are we? And in what time period?' she asked. 'And what was that blast?'

'The blast was our protection.' Mrs. M said from behind her. 'All transport sites have a protection device that explodes on the arrival of any unwanted visitors. We can never go back to the house in Dublin.' Gran added, holding her granddaughter's hand. The house is no longer there.' She took several long breaths before continuing.

'We must be in the forest surrounding Fotheringhay Castle. The date should be somewhere around February 1587. I just hope we did not overjump and miss our connection. You are going to see your mother. She is expecting you, but her time is short.'

‘Fotheringhay! That’s where she was beheaded!’ Mary Elizabeth gasped. ‘Are we here to stop it from happening?’

‘No child,’ Gran let out a deep sigh. ‘It is too late for that. But your mother has something for you and you need to speak to her, so she can help you on your journey to the throne of Scotland.’ She gave Mary Elizabeth hug. ‘That journey begins today.’

Mrs. M shushed them. ‘Someone is coming,’ she whispered.

‘Bonjour,’ a woman’s voice called out in French. ‘Is that you in there? Is that you, Queen Marie?’

‘Lady Jane,’ Is it you?’ Gran broke the silence, calling out, her French rolling off her tongue as if she had never spoken any other language.

‘Oui, my queen, Maire de Guise. It is I. Where are you?’

‘’Over here.’ Gran stood up and motioned for the others to do the same. ‘It is Lady Jane Kennedy, my daughter’s maid. We can trust her. She will take us to the queen.’

‘I thought my mother only surrounded herself with Mary’s.’ Mary Elizabeth noted.

‘She did, initially,’ Gran explained.

‘But time and situations changed. Her staff were cut when she was imprisoned here in England, and her household staff had to be approved by her cousin, Queen Elizabeth. If there was any doubt or concern about any of your mother’s attendants, they were dismissed, or worse, they disappeared.’

‘Executed?’

‘Most likely.’ Gran wrapped her arm around Mary Elizabeth and began to speak with urgency, determined to give her granddaughter as many words of wisdom as she could in a short amount of time.

'Speak clearly when you speak in English or French. No slang and under not circumstance, no swearing. You must now speak the lingo of the time you are in.'

'Yes Gran,' Mary Elizabeth answered, then corrected herself. 'I mean, Yes Grandmother.'

A shadow appeared. 'Come. We must move quickly.'

'Oui!' The conversation continued in old French and barely more that a whisper. If they were in Fotheringhay, then they were in the heart of England, the realm of Queen Elizabeth I, and she was well known to have her spies in every corner of her domain.

Gran took Mary Elizabeth's arm and linked it in hers, as they followed their guide, moving quickly. Lady Jane suddenly stopped and motioned silence. Everyone crouched down behind a thick hedge. The noise of horse's hooves where getting closer.

'She came this way,' a man's voice announced as the horses pulled up. 'We must track her, she may lead us to the queen's daughter.'

'Queen Mary, you mean? You cannot possibly believe that story of a young princess Mary Elizabeth that was whisked away at birth and then to return to claim her inheritance at the Scottish Queen's final hours.'

'I can, and I do believe that. I overheard Queen Mary herself, telling one of her maids that her daughter was coming to see her. The Scottish Queen maybe many things, but she is not one to fall for fanciful tales of missing princesses, unless the tale is based on truth. If there is a Scottish princess, Queen Elizabeth would reward us greatly for bringing her to court. Now let us go and find her, before she finds her way to her mother's side. We shall look this way and then turn back. Lady Jane could not have gone too far.'

Queen Elizabeth's men manoeuvred their horses around and set off.

'They will return.' Lady Jane stood up cautiously. 'We must make haste. Come, I know a back entrance and there are appropriate clothes for you to change into. We cannot have you walking around the castle looking like Scottish ladies, now can we?'

Lady Jane directed them around a corner, sheltered by tall hedges. She pulled open a big heavy door and ushered the ladies into the castle. She grabbed a lit torch from the wall and continued along a narrow passageway and made her way up some stairs.

'In here,' Lady Jane whispered as she stopped and pushed open a door that led to a tiny chamber. She proceeded to light the candles that were sitting on the ledge over the cold hearth.

'It is a storage room. I have all Her Majesty's gowns hanging here. Her chambers lack the space and she does not need them now. Not like she did when she ruled at Holyrood. Those were the grand days.' Lady Jane quickly wiped a tear from her eye, before turning to the ladies standing before her.

'I have just the gown for you.' She beamed at Mary Elizabeth.

'A gown fit for the princess that you are.' She reached for a lovely high neck lace gown with silver thread.

'Oh my!' Mary Elizabeth gasped.

'Take off your Scottish attire and slip this on. We will keep your things here until you leave.' Lady Jane handed Mary Elizabeth some light linen petticoats, decorated with small purple flowers. Then she quickly lifted the dress and slid it over Mary Elizabeth's head. She tugged at it lightly and the skirt fell to the floor. 'Turn around and I'll tighten the laces up the back.'

Mary Elizabeth could not help but feel like a princess.' It fits like a glove,' she noted. Lady Jane then opened a treasure box that sat on the ledge. 'Here,' she said. She reached around Mary Elizabeth and fastened a chain around her neck. A deep ruby crystal encased in a finely cut, silver mount.

'It belonged to your mother,' Gran said. 'I remember it well. I gave her that necklace. I sent it over to France shortly after she married the Dauphine. The dress is French lace. She sent me a miniature painting of her in the gown wearing the pendant. You look just like she did. Just like your mother.' Then turning to Lady Jane, she gave her a nod of approval.

Lady Jane stood back and looked at Mary Elizabeth. 'You are ready. I will take you to the queen.'

'I will stay here,' Mrs. M suggested. 'I will gather what we need from this room and will be prepared to leave when you return. Now go.'

CHAPTER THIRTEEN

Fotheringhay Castle

7th February 1587

She knelt in the corner at a small alter. Her fingers hastened over a long string of rosary beads, her head bowed in prayer. A single candle sat on one end of the alter, its flame casting a shadow of the crucifix against the wall.

She heard the door open but made no move to finish her prayers. A woman dressed in black stood up from where she knelt near the queen and indicated with a finger to her lips to stand quietly while they waited.

The minutes past and the queen continued to pray. She then made the sign of the cross and pushed herself off the kneeler before facing the ladies who where standing at the door.

'Enter,' she commanded in a soft voice. 'Lady Mary, stir the coals in the hearth and light some candles. We have much to discuss this night. It is my last night and I will not waste it with sleep.'

As Lady Mary followed her instructions, the queen motioned the others forward. 'Lady Jane.' She nodded towards their guide. 'You have found her. And my mother too. A job well done. Thank you.'

Lady Jane curtsied and stepped toward the hearth to assist Mary. 'Mother.' Queen Mary greeted her mother first. 'I still cannot understand this jaunting through time. I know you have explained it to me many times, but I still find it difficult to believe that you are my dearly departed mother. You died while I was in France and yet you still visit me, not looking a day older than myself. How can this be?' She waved her hand in front of her face. 'It does not matter. You are here now in my time of need. Come sit with me. I am weary of this world, weary of this life.'

The queen took at seat by the hearth. The flames flickering from the hearth caused shadows to cross the queen's face, making her look older than her forty-five years. Gran sat opposite her. Mary Elizabeth still standing by the door, not sure what to do.

'Come here child.' Queen Mary waved for Mary Elizabeth to come closer. 'I have waited a lifetime in captivity for this moment.'

Mary Elizabeth began moving slowly towards the queen, then stopped and presented her most graceful curtsy.

The queen reached for her hand and placed it in hers. 'You look just like I did once. So young, so beautiful. And to think that you almost did not live. You were so tiny when I held you in Loch Leven Castle. But you were there too, were you not? You were the young lady who rescued, yourself as a tiny baby, are you not?'

'Yes, Your Majesty,' Mary Elizabeth answered with respect.

'You must call me mother.' Queen Mary insisted. 'For that is what I am, your mother. And, at least for tonight, we can be mother and daughter. For tomorrow they will execute me for crimes I did not commit.'

'No,' Mary Elizabeth could not stop her groan.

'I have always wanted to meet my mother. Grandmother always told me that my mother was dead.'

'And I suppose you could say that,' Gran pointed out, 'that in the 21st century you mother was dead. And had been for quite a few centuries, at least.'

Mary Elizabeth blushed at her grandmother's wit. She was truthful to a fault.

The Queen of Scots studied her daughter fondly. 'Your grandmother always did have a way of making truths out of non-truths. That does not matter now. What matters now is that I prepare you as best I can for the life you will lead. You will be queen – a queen like no other, of that I am sure.' She motioned to one of her other Mary's. 'Another chair please. We have much to discuss and I cannot have my daughter standing beside me all night.'

Mary Elizabeth nodded her thanks and sat beside her mother.

'My brother.' Mary Elizabeth looked confused. 'He is the King of Scotland. And someday he will rule both Scotland and England.'

'You are assuming my cousin will name him her heir,' Queen Mary said.

'Perhaps she does not have anyone. But I suppose you already know what happens.'

Mary Elizabeth nodded. 'And it is not good for Scotland. Not now and not in the future. In the 21st century, the Scottish people are fighting for their independence.

Queen Mary looked up. 'Is that what happens?'

Both Mary Elizabeth and her grandmother nodded.

'Well then, my dear daughter, you have your work cut out for you. But of course, there is no guaranteeing that what you do in your lifetime as Queen Mary Elizabeth of Scotland will affect much, if any, of the future. Your descendants may choose to join England, or one of James' descendants may do battle and reclaim Scotland. All you can do is make things right for now and hope for the best for the future.

Queen Mary reached across and grasped Mary Elizabeth's hand. 'You my dear child must be strong. I know mother has taught you well in all that you need to know, but some things cannot be taught. Learn from my mistakes. Never let your heart rule. Always rule with your head. And trust no one. Especially a man. All they want is to claim your kingdom for themselves.

Mary Elizabeth gasped. She hadn't expected her mother, a 16th century monarch to talk so rashly.

'I am sorry to say, it is the truth.' Queen Mary released her daughter's hand. 'I have allowed my heart to rule, first with Francois, my childhood sweetheart, then with that Darnley fellow, worst mistake I made, and finally with your father, the strong and rugged Scotsman, who adored me or at least I thought he did at the time. I believe he was quite insane when he died. I have kept my faith and that is all that has kept me sane.' She gazed into the flames. 'You will be a great queen, my darling daughter. Much greater than our cousin, Elizabeth. Do not allow anyone to get the better of you. Be strong. Be sure. And be ever true to your faith.'

'I can tell my mother has taught you well in French. You speak it fluently and obviously understand it well. Can you read French?' Mary Elizabeth nodded. The queen turned and waved her hand at Lady Mary who then brought over a casket and handed it to the queen. She pulled out a sheet of paper, marked with elegant penmanship, and handed it to her daughter. 'Read it to me.'

'You wrote this?' Mary Elizabeth asked. The queen nodded and waved at the young woman to proceed with her instructions. Mary Elizabeth obliged and started to read the French passage with ease.

'Now translate it into English,' Queen Mary insisted.

'8th February 1587, Sire, my brother-in-law, having by God's will, for my sins I think, thrown myself into the power of the queen, my cousin, at whose hands I have suffered much for almost twenty years, I have finally been condemned to death by her and her estate. I have asked for my papers, which they have taken away, in order that I might make my will, but I have not been able to recover anything of use to me, or even get leave, either to make my will freely or to have my body conveyed after my death, as I would wish to your kingdom where I had the honour to be queen, your sister and old ally.

Tonight, after dinner. I have been advised of my sentence: I am to be executed like a criminal at eight in the morning. I have not had time to give a full account.....'

'Enough,' the queen stopped the recitation bluntly. 'This letter will be sent to the King of France. There are others. You may read them all and learn from them. There are some in Latin. You do speak and read Latin? Mary Elizabeth nodded. 'Good. And you speak Gaelic, I understand.' Mary Elizabeth nodded again. 'I should have taken the time to learn the native tongue of my people.'

She patted Mary Elizabeth's hand affectionately and took back the letter, folding it carefully before locking it away in the casket. Lady Mary then handed the Queen a large leather bag and the queen placed the casket inside and handed it to her daughter.

'Take this. Read it all and keep it safe until all the letters have been delivered as they should be. And remember to rule with your head not your heart, although your heart should reach out to your subjects and, at all cost, put them and their well-being before your own.

'You must go now.' Queen Mary eventually said. She stood up slowly. Mary Elizabeth and her grandmother stood up after her. 'I must prepare to meet my Creator, and you must be far away when the sword falls, so that they cannot imprison you for life as they did to me!'

The queen took her daughter in her arms and embraced her warmly.

'Oh! How I have missed doing this over the years. I missed watching you grow up into the beautiful woman that you are now. Go! Before it is too late.'

Turning to Gran, she hugged her mother. 'You too, must go. You still have work to do, helping my daughter, your granddaughter, to be the leader she was meant to be and to save our Scotland.'

'I would stay,' Gran tried to say, but Queen Mary shook her head. Gran nodded in understanding. Mary Elizabeth put the leather bag over her head as she forced herself to walk away from her mother, who she had only just met.

Lady Jane escorted the two women out of the queen's chambers. Mary Elizabeth could not resist glancing back one last time. The queen was already back on her knees, in front of the alter.

CHAPTER FOURTEEN

As the ladies made their way to the stairs, they heard footsteps coming their way.

'This way.' A man came out of the shadows. 'Come quickly. They know you are in the castle, Princess.'

The women did not argue. The footsteps were getting closer, then they heard voices calling out commands.

'To the Queen's chamber.'

'Do not let her escape.'

The ladies didn't stop to think about their options, choosing to follow the mysterious man from the shadows. It was a risk, but what alternative did they have. As they got closer to see the man's face, Mary Elizabeth let out a gasp.

'Jamie? I thought'...She couldn't finish. Jamie waved his hand to shush her. He opened a door at the end of the hall and shoved them all inside. 'Put this on.' He told Mary Elizabeth as he handed her the cloak. 'Mrs. Murphy insisted I bring this for you. Who knows where we will end up. We have-to leave now, they will be here in a minute. Lady Jane, you get back to the queen.'

Jamie faced Lady Jane. 'As soon as you can, find Mrs. Murphy and tell her we will meet up with her at the safe house.' Lady Jane nodded and headed back to the queen's chambers.

Jamie moved closer to the corner where Mary Elizabeth and Gran were huddled. Everything went black just as the door that separated them from the English soldiers burst open.

All the sounds from the castle disappeared as an engine sounded and they were met by flashing car lights. 'Where are we?' Mary Elizabeth asked. 'Sometime in the 21st century. We are in Northamptonshire.'

'What now?' Gran asked.

'Well, the castle no longer exists.' Jamie was very blunt. 'All that remains is a huge mound where the castle once stood and a couple of markers that indicate its historical significance. That is the fate of most of the castles in England and Scotland. Mrs. Murphy has already made her escape and we will return to her shortly in the 16th century. We had best move off the road and make our way into the woods.'

The women did as they were told. They were too tired to argue. Jamie turned, 'beyond the trees is a pasture full of horses. We will need those horses for our escape and our jump back in time. Mrs. Murphy is waiting for us, not far away.'

'In this time or the past?' Mary Elizabeth asked. 'I am so dizzy from all this jumping through time.'

'We are going back to the past.' Jamie answered.

'It is not an exact science,' Gran explained. 'And not everyone is capable of time travel. That is why we left Lady Jane behind. She is not a time traveller, although she does believe in it.'

Mary Elizabeth was surprised that both her mother and one of her ladies, women of the 16th century believed in time travel. It was something that even the people of the 21st century had difficulty believing.

Jamie spoke, breaking Mary Elizabeth thoughts. 'We must hurry.'

They broke through the far end of the forest and noticed the horses waiting. 'The white one is for the Princess. Let us make haste, we have no time to lose. Just follow my lead and we'll be back with Mrs. Murphy in no time.' The women followed Jamie easily, their horses were eager to keep up with the one in the lead.

As Mary Elizabeth looked ahead, she noticed the sun had risen. 'What time is it?' she asked.

'Almost eight o'clock, I believe,' Gran said.

Mary choked back a sob. She knew that she was standing in a time over 400 hundred years later, but she had only just met her mother in the past and now the hour of her death, in her time period was approaching.

'Ave Maria, gratia plena, Dominus tecum

Benedicta tu in mulieribus, et Benedictus

Fructus ventris tui, Iessus.

Sancta Maria,

Mater Dei, ora pro nobis peccatoribus

Nunc, et in hora mortis nostrae. Amen.'

The voice was just like a whisper, the Latin words washed over the princess as she listened intently to the voice in her head.

'Hail Mary, full of grace,

The Lord is with dee.

Blessed art thou among women

And blessed is the fruit of thy womb, Jesus

Holy Mary, mother of God,

Pray for us sinners, now and at the hour of our death

Amen.'

A man's voice was then heard 'In nominee Patris et Filii et Spiritus Sancti, Amen.'

A shadow then crossed Mary Elizabeth's eyes as a hand made the sign of the cross.

'Pater Noster,' the Latin continued with the voices of a man and a woman together. The man's voice faded and then Mary Elizabeth heard the voice that she had only heard hours before. 'I hope you will spare me and make it quick.'

A swoosh.

'Ave Maria, gratia plena, Dominus .....'

The voice was halted mid-prayer with a snap.

'NO!!!' Mary Elizabeth screamed.

'Princess.' Jamie reached across to where Mary Elizabeth was seated on her horse, her head in her hands.

'She's gone!' she jumped from her thoughts.

'I heard her last prayers. She begged the executioner to make it quick.' Tears flowed down her cheeks.

'I know, but we must be gone from this place and this time.' Jamie pointed across the field. 'We must go now. Back to the past.'

As they made their way out of the forest, the horses slowed into a trot. 'Where and when are we now?' Mary Elizabeth studied her surroundings once again, trying to recognise something familiar.

'We are back in 1587 and we are just outside Fotheringhay.' Jamie told them before nudging his horse into a canter.

After another hour had past, Jamie pointed ahead. 'There's a cottage just over the hill. Mrs. Murphy should be waiting for us there. Then we must depart immediately before we are found by our pursuers.

'NO!' Mary Elizabeth spoke up surprising herself as well as the others. We will not keep running. We cannot run forever.'

'I agree with my granddaughter.' Gran nodded to Mary Elizabeth.

As they pulled their horses to a stop outside the cottage, Mrs. M came running out to greet them. 'Mrs. M,' Mary Elizabeth gasped in relief. 'I was not sure I would ever see you again. We left you stranded in Fotheringhay.'

'Not quite stranded.' The older woman fondly acknowledged the princess. 'Lady Jane came to my rescue and helped me escape the castle. I managed to bring your things and other treasures. But you are exhausted, and I am sure you are all hungry, we can talk inside while you eat.'

It was a relief to enter the warmth of the cottage. The hearth glowed bright and had a large pot of stew hanging over the flames, waiting for them. They did not need much urging. They washed quickly and found a seat on the bench that ran the length of the table.

'Mistress Douglas,' Mrs. M announced making the introductions, may I present James Stuart, Earl of Moray.' Jamie gave a slight bow. 'My lady, Queen Mother, Marie de Guise, and her Royal Highness, Princess Mary Elizabeth of Scotland.'

Their hostess gave an awkward curtsy and welcomed them to her humble home. They all remained quiet, while they enjoyed their hot bowls of stew and bread.

Jamie looked across at Mary Elizabeth. 'How are you feeling now that you are fed?'

Mary Elizabeth smiled up at him. 'A lot better, thank you, but of course, so confused as to why people are chasing me.'

'They want to stop you,' Jamie snapped. 'They feel threatened by you and your purpose.'

'Stop me from what? Threatened why?'

'From keeping Scotland independent,' James answered bluntly. 'Now enough, get some rest.'

'Why does he do that? Why does he order me about like that? If I ask a question, I expect to get an answer.'

Gran laughed. 'I think he likes you a little more than you realise.' She patted her granddaughter on the arm with affection. 'and what he feels for you is making him overly protective of you.'

Mrs. M appeared and motioned for Mary Elizabeth to follow her into the back room. 'I have lots of clothes here for you. Some used to be your mother's. Lady Jane helped me move them from the castle.'

'We should wear dark colours, in respect for my daughter.' Gran said.

'Were you there, Mrs. M?' Mary Elizabeth had to ask. 'Were you with my mother when she was…' She couldn't bring herself to say that dreadful word, beheaded.

'Yes, dear,' Mrs. M replied in a whisper. 'I was there. Among the crowd, I stood at the back. I did not want to be there, but I had to meet Lady Jane. I had not meant to witness the sad demise of your mother, princess, but I was pulled along by the crowd.'

'I met up with Lady Jane later that day. She was obviously distraught. Not just for the death of her mistress, but also because

Queen Elizabeth has ordered that Queen Mary's attendants be arrested on multiple counts of treason.'

'What?' Mary Elizabeth couldn't believe what she was hearing. How could Queen Elizabeth treat her cousin's attendants as criminals? 'That is outrageous!' Mary Elizabeth started pacing the floor.

'I must do something. I must go and see my cousin, the queen.' The other women all shook their heads at the same time. But Mary Elizabeth crossed her arms like she did when she was a young girl, determined to get what she wanted. 'I will see her. And I will insist on their releases!'

Her insistence was met with silence. Gran was the first to break it.

'And how will you manage to obtain an audience with the queen? The Mrs. M followed, 'she will not believe your claim. She will have you arrested, thrown in the tower and beheaded like your mother.'

Tears started to run down the young princess's face. She couldn't take it anymore. First, she started travelling through time and witnessed her own birth then she met her mother for the first and only time, who turned out to be Mary Queen of Scots. Nothing made sense.

Mary Elizabeth dropped to her knees. 'I will go, and I will see her!'

Gran sat down on the floor beside her, 'Fine, dear. We will meet up with your army and make the plans.'

Mary Elizabeth looked up rubbing her eyes. 'My army? What army?'

Jamie will explain. But for now, you need to rest.'

'I want to see my father, too.' Mary Elizabeth said. Gran had started to get up, when her granddaughter's comment stopped her. 'He is dead, you know.' She turned to face Mary Elizabeth. 'And you have met your father already, long ago.' Do you remember that time you had a nightmare and you were in a dark room with a scary man with a beard who claimed to be your father?' Mary Elizabeth nodded as she remembered that terrifying night when she was about eight or nine years old. 'That was no nightmare, that was your first adventure in time travel.'

'I remember he mentioned something about an inheritance.' Mary Elizabeth started to remember. 'Something about a castle, his castle. That it would help me finance my battle. I did not understand what he was talking about at the time, but now I must go to Bothwell Castle? Or is it Dunbar Castle? Where he kept my mother safe?'

Mary Elizabeth went to rest and read her mother's papers. As well as checking out what Mrs. M had brought back from Fotheringhay with her.

Gran sat with her awhile. 'We shall make our way north to Northumberland in the morning, to Alnwick Castle, the seat of the Duke of Northumberland.'

'I thought my cousin had Thomas Percy executed back in 1572, was it? Because he was supporting my mother.'

'All true.' Gran smiled at her.

'You remembered your history lessons well. The English queen has confiscated Northumberland's titles and estates, but there are still supporters, not to mention his son, another Thomas. All that said, for now it is the safest castle to launch your campaign.'

'My campaign?'

'Well for starters, I thought you wanted to confront, Queen Elizabeth?'

'I do!' Mary Elizabeth agreed. 'I must meet her and secure the release of my mother's attendants. I also want to make her aware of my existence and the threat I pose for her.'

'All in good time, my child.' Gran gave Mary Elizabeth a tight hug and left her to rest.

CHAPTER FIFTEEN

Dragsholm Castle, Denmark

April 1578

'Come here, child.' It sounded like Gran's voice – soft and compassionate – but there was an echo in this tiny, dark room. There was only one window, so small that no light could possibly light the room from the outside.

Mary Elizabeth's feet moved, pulling her forward. Her grandmother was beckoning her forward toward a bench. There she saw what looked like a lump of rags lying on the bench. The rags moved, and Mary Elizabeth jumped and ran to hide behind her grandmother.

'Marie de Guise, as I live and breathe,' the lump of rags spoke in a deep voice. It sat up and hands moved up to rub its eyes. 'I thought you were dead. All these years and here you are before me. May as well be, now that your daughter is imprisoned. And for what?' he let out a sob. 'So that she could love a man like me, and a good Scotsman at that.'

'Ah, James. My dear Lord Bothwell.' Gran let out a deep sigh and Mary Elizabeth peeked out from behind her. She was small for her age, but she always felt safe when she was close to her grandmother. 'Always my faithful lord. The only one who stood up for my daughter, the only Scotsman who tried to keep her safe.'

'I did try, did I not?' There was a glimmer of hope in his eyes. 'How is she?' Still imprisoned by that wicked Queen of England?'

'Aye, my Lord,' Gran said with sadness in her voice. 'But she still loves you, you know. She remains faithful to you, a love she never thought she could truly have, being the lonely queen of a country divided by religious factions.'

Lord Bothwell nodded in agreement, with sadness in his eyes. He looked directly at the young child who was hiding.

'And who is the child?'

'Your daughter, Mary Elizabeth.' Gran reached behind her and pushed the girl forward. 'Mary Elizabeth, you have always wondered about your parents. This is your father, James Hepburn, Lord Bothwell, your mother's last husband.'

'Queen Mary's daughter?' Lord Bothwell studied the young girl. 'But they told me the baby was born dead.'

'One was, but there were two, and we kept this one safe. For Scotland.'

'For Scotland.' Lord Bothwell struggled to believe what was happening but managed to smile at the girl looking back at him. He held out his hand to his daughter. 'Come here, Mary Elizabeth. Come sit with an old man and tell me about yourself. I do not have long to live, but I know I will die a happy man having made your acquaintance.'

Mary Elizabeth walked across the room towards him. 'Are you my father?'

'That is what your grandmother says,' Lord Bothwell replied. 'You look like your mother, but you also have the strong blood of a pure Scotsman. You will be a force to be reckoned with, and you will

make your family and your homeland strong and proud.' He looked up at Gran. 'For Scotland.'

'Aye, for Scotland.'

Mary Elizabeth sat beside her father, studying him closely, taking note of his long scraggly beard.

'Tis is the life I now lead. I was once a grand lord in your mother's court, and before that in your grandmother's court.'

'In Scotland?'

'Aye, in Scotland. And how old are you now, my little princess?' he asked her softly. Gran stood in the centre of the room, watching the interaction between her granddaughter and her son-in-law.

'Eleven,' she answered. 'At least I will be eleven in the summer.'

'Eleven years, has it been that long? She was a good woman, your mother, and a good queen. She was never given a chance. Her half-brother, the Earl of Moray, made sure of that. He was jealous of her. He felt he deserved the crown being the last King's son. But he was illegitimate, you see. Although there were those that claimed Queen Elizabeth was also illegitimate and she became queen. Does she rule still?'

He looked up at Gran. She nodded. 'Aye, both Queen Elizabeth and Queen Mary are still alive. My daughter continues to be her prisoner, but she is kept in much better rooms than this, my lord.'

Lord Bothwell sadly nodded. 'That is good. She would not fare well in a place like this.' He let out a deep sigh of frustration as he looked down at his child.

A bang came to the door and startled the young girl. She ran for cover back behind her grandmother. 'What goes on in there?' a man's voice called out. 'You talking to yourself again Bothwell?'

'Aye!' Lord Bothwell yelled back. His expression was full of sadness as he gave Gran and his daughter a weak smile. 'A bonny lass for Scotland.'

'Aye!' Gran agreed.

'Help her find my inheritance. It will support her campaign.' His words faded as did the room and the man.

'For Scotland!'

CHAPTER SIXTEEN

Mary Elizabeth woke the following morning with a start, the remnants of her dream was causing her some confusion. As if reading her mind, her grandmother appeared and sat down beside her.

'I had a dream last night.'

'I thought you might have.' Gran took her hand. 'Were you with your father?'

'Aye', Mary said, pleased with herself for taking up the familiar Scottish word for agreement. 'I was just a little girl. Eleven.'

'That is about right.' Gran nodded. 'It was just before your father died. He rotted in that prison. So sad. But I do believe he died happy knowing that you lived and that you would one day be the ruler he had hoped your mother would be. It is your destiny, child.'

They both got up at the sound of Jamie's voice. 'The horses are ready, we must go.' Jamie instructed.

'But what about the Douglas'?' Mary Elizabeth asked. 'We cannot leave them here.'

'They have chosen to come with us. They want to serve you, Mary Elizabeth. They would like to see you on the throne of Scotland.'

'But what about my brother, King James?'

'Our lady of questions,' Jamie laughed.

'And you are not the regent, are you?' Mary Elizabeth stared at him. 'What I do not know is, who are you?'

'You are right, princess,' Jamie looked at her fondly, sending blushes to her cheeks.

'I am not the regent, James Stuart, Earl of Moray. I am his nephew, James Stuart, Earl of Moray, partially by inheritance, but also for my devoted service to your half-brother the king. A service I have decided to sever in the future but will remain in active duty in the past.

'So, we are related,' Mary Elizabeth surmised.

'But you are not my uncle?'

'No, I am not your uncle and we are not closely related,' Jamie tried to explain. 'My father was your uncle, the regent's half-brother. You will recall from your studies that your grandfather liked to play around, so to speak.'

'Yes, Yes.' Mary Elizabeth waved her hand. 'I get the connection. Spare me the sordid details.'

'Does he know that you are fighting for me now, instead of him? Does he know you are fighting for his downfall?'

'You are referring to your brother, I presume.'

The princess nodded.

'Well I am not exactly fighting for his downfall.' Jamie elaborated. Then Gran decided to intervene. 'We will not overturn King James VI. All we plan to do is make sure that when he accepts the crown of England, he leaves Scotland to you. That way Scotland will remain an independent country.'

With that, Mrs. M arrived with her bundles of clothes to take with them. Mary Elizabeth followed her grandmother to retrieve their weapons and her mother's treasured box before joining everyone outside. Once outside she noticed all the horses were saddled. There was a small cart loaded with bundles of clothes, food and all their personal effects. They were ready to leave.

'How long will it take to reach Northumberland?' the princess asked Jamie.

'Depends on the weather, but all going well, perhaps just under two weeks.'

'Two weeks!' Mary Elizabeth exclaimed.

'In that case, I have to turn around and make my way back south to confront Elizabeth. That's much too long. Why can't we go see my cousin first?'

'Because your army is waiting in Northumberland. You will never be safe in England without an army at your back.' Jamie explained, patiently.

Mrs. M came over to stand beside her. She handed Mary Elizabeth a long cloak lined with fur. 'This will keep you warm and appropriately covered while you ride.' Mary Elizabeth accepted it and wrapped it around her shoulders. Mrs. M then helped drape the length of the cloak over the horse.

'One last thing. You must no longer refer to me as Mrs. M. That was the name I adopted for the 21st century. As your Grandmother's personal maid and closest friend, I was well revered in the 16th century as Lady Mary Catherine de Guise. I am your Grandmother's cousin, another of the Guise clan.'

'And another Mary. My Mary Catherine de Guise. Mary Elizabeth bowed her head in acknowledgement and Lady Mary Catherine honoured her with a curtsy.

CHAPTER SEVENTEEN

STIRLING CASTLE, 1587

'Your Majesty,' the messenger said, down on one knee and bowed his head. 'A message from the borders, your majesty.' He handed it to George Gordon, sixth Earl of Huntly. The Earl then stepped up and handed it to the King.

'Your Majesty.' He bowed and returned to his position at the bottom of the steps. He may be the king's closest friend, and if the rumours where true, his lover, but he had to keep up appearances in public. King James held the sealed note in his hands, wondering its importance.

It was a lovely summers day and the last thing the king wanted to do was attend to more missives. He wanted to enjoy himself while at Stirling. He had some fond memories of this place, it being his childhood home. He wanted to get out on the grounds and enjoy some outdoor pursuits while the weather was good, but duty came first.

With a deep sigh, he broke the seal and opened the missive. After a quick glance he threw it on the floor, stood up and stomped on it with contempt.

'What is it, you Majesty?' the Earl asked, while he knelt forward to retrieve the letter before it was destroyed.

'Read it, if you must,' the king snapped. 'She is at the border. In Northumberland.'

'Who is, your Majesty?'

'Who do you think, the one who claims to be my sister. The one claiming to be Princess Mary Elizabeth, second in line to the throne of Scotland. The nerve!'

'Is it possible, my lord?' The Earl nervously asked.

'No! It cannot be!' The King stormed back and forth in front of his throne. 'They say the baby died at birth. But then, they also said the baby was a boy.'

'Could there have been two babies?' Francis Stuart Hepburn, Earl of Bothwell, (a title reassigned after Queen Mary's Lord Bothwell died in prison) appearing at the side of the king.

'Could your mother have given birth to twins?'

'If she had, why was there no record?' The king continued. 'And where has she been all these years? And now she appears after I hear the news that my mother has been beheaded at Fotheringhay. It just does not make any sense.'

The Earl of Huntly studied the missive, reading it carefully. He hesitated before repeating what he had read. 'They say she looks like your mother.'

'That does not mean she is my sister.' King James roared. 'This is just another plot, it has to be. She cannot be my sister, can she? And even if she is, what is it she wants from me?'

'She wants to take your throne. It is obvious. She thinks she can do better than you.'

'Better than me? I am the most learned monarch in all of Christendom?' James shouted back his response.

'No! There is no one better than I to rule this land. I am the King of Scotland. It is my divine right to rule this country.'

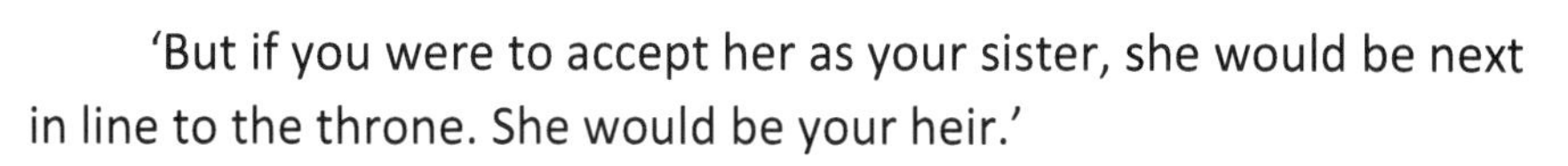

'But if you were to accept her as your sister, she would be next in line to the throne. She would be your heir.'

'Well then. I must marry. I must have children. That will block her line of succession.'

'Do you think she is your sister?'

'I do not know,' the king said sadly. 'As much as I would like to believe I have a sibling and we could be reunited, it is only wishful thinking. I just do not know what to think.'

CHAPTER EIGHTEEN

GREENWICH CASTLE, 1587

'What is it Robbie?' She stood at the window of her private chambers, looking out at the grass glistening in the rain. Even though it was summertime, the cold rain would not ease up. It was as if she was being punished. Maybe she was. She had done some horrible things, the latest being the execution of her Scottish cousin.

Her grandfather and even her father had been ruthless and brutal in their executions. She did not want to be remembered for that. But then, she had signed the document and the deed was done. Now she must suffer.

Her mother had stood at these very windows, probably wondering her own fate at one time. Her father, King Henry VIII, had been a volatile King with uncontrollable mood swings, especially when it came to women. And the notion her father had about needing a male heir. Rubbish. She was and would be remembered as a great queen, she thought to herself. Unlike her weak, sickly brother, Edward, who had only lived a few years as king.

She, Elizabeth, had watched and waited. She had learned how to survive and how to manipulate and now, in so many ways she was her father all over again.

'Robbie'. Her eyes moved away from the window and gazed at her one and only true love, the man who would do anything for her,

Robert Dudley, Earl of Leicester. He had asked her to marry him and she nearly accepted, several times, but duty interfered. Either she married a foreign prince, or she remained single and ruled on her own. She felt stronger that way.

'What is it Robbie, you look worried?'

'I am, your Majesty.' Bessie, my dearest. She is coming. And she is coming with a mighty army and vengeance in her heart for her mother.'

'So, it is true. My cousin has another child, and a girl, no doubt.' And what do we call her?'

'Princess Mary Elizabeth,' Robbie handed her over the missive.

Queen Elizabeth I, not always liked, opened the document and read it quickly before tossing it on the floor and began trampling on it with her foot. She was angry now. 'She wants to meet with me.' The queen screamed at Robbie as if it was his fault. 'No! She demands to meet with me! How dare she! How dare this little creature, claiming to be Queen Mary's daughter demand to meet with the mightiest ruler of all time. I do NOT have to bow to her whims. I do NOT have to meet her demands. I do NOT have to meet with her. Did I ever agree to meet her mother, NO! and I shall not meet with her either. WHO DOES SHE THINK SHE IS?'

The storm of words continued for some time. 'I will not, Robbie, I will not!'

CHAPTER NINETEEN

NORTHERN ENGLAND, 1587

'I can hear them all in my head, in my dreams and when I am awake.' Mary Elizabeth told Gran. 'They are not happy, they are stunned to say the least, and very angry.

'Who?' Gran asked, although she must have known.

'My brother and my cousin, the King of Scotland and the Queen of England.' Mary Elizabeth let out a sigh. 'I feel like I am a fly on their walls in their private chambers. Any time they discuss me, I am there. I do not understand it.'

'But you will be better prepared by the experience.' Gran pointed out the obvious. 'You'll know what to expect.'

When the group had arrived in Northumberland, an army was standing by, ready to march, and growing in numbers every day. Now rested, Mary Elizabeth was ready to finally make her way south. She had a task to do. She insisted on meeting with her cousin face to face.

From reading up on her history in the 21st century, Mary Elizabeth knew that her mother, Queen Mary of Scotland had requested numerous times to meet with Elizabeth, but Elizabeth always refused. Too scared maybe? But Mary Elizabeth was not going to give her cousin the option. If an audience was not granted, Mary Elizabeth knew of a few ways to catch the queen by surprise and unannounced. As she thought about it, the element of surprise had a spark of justice to it, especially with the special gift she was carrying to give to the English Queen.

There had been missives waiting for her when she had arrived at Alnwick Castle. Not from her brother and certainly not from her cousin. These missives where from across the north of England and into the Scottish Highlands, with lords pledging their allegiance to her as heir to the Scottish throne. She could not believe it. It wasn't that long ago that she was sitting at her desk at home in Dublin writing on her history blog. Now it seemed she would become a person of interest in the history books of Scotland as well as England.

She was concerned on how she was going to pay her soldiers. There were at least a thousand or more. She couldn't bear the thought of starting her reign with a huge debt. Gran waved aside her concerns. 'I have a little money, and when that runs out, there is always your father's treasure.'

'If we can find it,' the princess pointed out. She would have to be content with her grandmother's reasoning for now. If there was money for the present mounting expenses, that was all that mattered. And they could not go looking for Lord Bothwell's treasure anytime soon. She was dealing with Queen Elizabeth before she did anything else.

They continued to ride in silence, enjoying the warmth of the sunlight. The time had passed quickly since she had first met her mother, but she had seen her again. She had jumped back in time during evenings when she knew Queen Mary was alone. Mary Elizabeth had visited her in the various castles of her lengthy captivity in England. First in Dunbrennan Abbey, where the queen had only stayed one night, after her escape from the battle of Langside. Then when the queen crossed over into England, staying at Workington Hall, then Carlisle Castle. It had been interesting, and

Mary Elizabeth saw another side of her mother, one that was missed by the historians. She was not the weak, tragic woman that fell for any man. She was dedicated to her purpose, seeking her cousin, Queen Elizabeth's help in regaining her throne in Scotland. Which was not to be. In fact, the English queen moved Queen Mary further away from the Scottish border to prevent an uprising in the north.

Mary Elizabeth jumped back in time many times. She spent a good bit of time at Bolton Castle where her mother spent six months. After that the Queen was moved to Tutbury Castle, then Sheffield Castle, Wingfield Manor and Chatsworth House.

Each time she was moved, her staff were reduced. As Mary Elizabeth visited her mother in each of these prisons, she was heartbroken to witness the growing look of defeat overtake the Scottish Queen. Remembering her last visit with her mother, Mary Elizabeth started humming a tune she had heard her mother sing. Without realising Mary Elizabeth began reciting the words out loud:

Lord, grant your mercy unto me

Teach me some way that he may know

My love for him is no an empty show

But purest tenderness and constancy

For does he not, alas, ev'n now possess

This body and this heart which would not flee

Discord, dishonour nor uncertainty.

'Your mother wrote that, did she not?' Gran asked, interrupting the princess. Mary Elizabeth nodded.

'Aye, it is one of her sonnets. She wrote quite a few.' The princess replied. 'Some are in the papers that she left me.'

'She was quite talented.' Her grandmother said.

Jamie galloped back from the front of the troop, interrupting their conversation. 'We will be camping just beyond that village. I have sent men ahead to set up.' Looking at the princess, he added, 'You are a day ride from London. We need to plan ahead.'

'Perhaps we should just go straight to Greenwich.' Mary Elizabeth suggested. 'She is always there with her court, it is her favourite palace.'

'I suppose you have been there as well.' Gran said.

Mary Elizabeth smiled and said, 'I am a fly on the wall, remember?' Gran shook her head, 'I should have known.' Gran knew that since her granddaughter knew about her talent for time-travel she had been jumping from this time to the next. 'Just be careful.'

'Yes Grandmother.'

'So, tell me about it. Have you learned anything interesting about the English queen, who people say never ages.' She princess laughed. 'She does age Grandmother. She just dresses so outrageously and plasters her face with white powder so no-one can see the wrinkles on her face. Ridiculous, if you ask me.'

'And I hear she always wears white, to reinforce her image as the Virgin Queen.'

Mary Elizabeth snorted. I am quite sure she is anything but a virgin, Grandmother. I'll say no more.' Mary Elizabeth laughed.

CHAPTER TWENTY

FOTHERINGHAY CASTLE

8TH FEBRUARY 1587

'Take my gloves. Take my rosary. Give them to my cousin. But first I will take these things with me as I lay my head on the block and prepare to meet my Creator.

She allowed her lady's maid pull on her favourite gloves. She had already dressed in her gown and cape. She was handed her beads just as a knock on the door came, signalling the time. 'After the deed is done.' She nodded. It was time. She stood with her ladies, wiping away their tears that ran down their faces before giving them a hug. Queens did not usually hug their ladies, but these were unusual circumstances and she was no ordinary Queen.

She thanked each of her ladies in turn and faced the guard, who stood waiting to escort her. The group walked in unison and then paused briefly when they reached the door to the courtyard. It was a dull day, in every sense.

'It is time,' the queen said. She told her ladies to wait by the door. She would walk the last few steps and mount the scaffold with only the guard and confessor.

Mounting the scaffold, she offered her forgiveness to the executioner. Then the confessor blessed her. She removed her cloak and handed it to him. She kept her gloves on and her rosary beads moved quickly through her fingers. Then she knelt-down at the block and lay her neck on its surface.

The swoosh of the blade was swift, but it just bounced off the back of her neck. Her voice was still whispering her prayers. She heard a second swoosh and felt the impact again on her neck. She was still breathing and still praying.

'Take me, Lord,' she almost cried out, but her disciplined voice continued with her prayers. She could feel the trickle of warm blood flow down the back of her neck. The swoosh came again, the third stroke. Her eyes jolted open for one last glimpse of what she was leaving behind. Her head rolled, leaving her body and the blood splattered on her gown and gloves.

CHAPTER TWENTY-ONE

APPROACHING LONDON 1587

Lights glowed inside the main tent when Jamie, Gran, Lady Mary Catherine and Lord Thomas Percy, the unrecognised Earl of Northumberland had gathered.

'You cannot just walk in there like a visiting royal cousin.' Jamie pointed out.

'But that is just it, I am a visiting royal cousin.' The princess replied quickly.

'But she does not believe you, your Highness.' Young Thomas muttered. 'All of our spies say the same thing. Queen Elizabeth believes you to be a fraud.'

'No more than her grandfather, Henry VII.' Mary Elizabeth knew her history and she knew it well. She stared intently at each one in turn. 'I will take six of your finest soldiers along with Jamie and Lady Mary Catherine. Grandmother you stay here with Lord Thomas and if something goes wrong and the queen decides to lock me in the tower, you must come to my aid.'

'Lord Thomas, if something does go wrong and I do not return, you must send the rest of my army south. Now we must all get some sleep, for tomorrow will be a busy day.'

CHAPTER TWENTY-TWO

GREENWICH CASTLE 1587

'It sounds rather noisy in there, does it not?' Mary Elizabeth asked the queen's guard, who held the door. 'I wonder what they're all arguing about? Me perhaps?'

The guard said nothing but the twitch at the corners of his lips suggested he wanted to smile.

'Perhaps you should announce me, and we shall see what happens next.' The princess gave him her prettiest smile, followed by a wink.

The guard blushed as he opened the doors. 'Her Royal Highness, the Princess Mary Elizabeth of Scotland, daughter of the late Mary, Queen of Scotland and her husband Lord Bothwell, granddaughter of King James V of Scotland and his wife Marie de Guise. Cousin of our Queen, Elizabeth I of England.'

Mary had insisted on the full account of her ancestry. The guard had hesitated until Jamie handed him several gold coins.

The silence that greeted his announcement was not surprising. All the faces turned to see the Scottish Princess who had suddenly appeared out of nowhere and who dared show up at the English court to face the English Queen. The lords and ladies parted, creating a path down the centre of the room. As Mary Elizabeth walked forward, with her head held high and a look of determination on her face, she saw the far end of the room and the scowling face of the Queen of England.

She maintained her composure and locked eyes with her cousin. She felt reassured that Jamie was nearby and armed. There was no sound but the rustle of her gown. She reached the dais and paused before executing a perfect curtsy. 'Your Majesty,' she said loud and clear with grace and conviction. 'Cousin.'

The queen grimaced at Mary Elizabeth's final greeting. 'How dare you!' she snarled. It appeared that the princess's presence was trying Queen Elizabeth's infamous temper. 'How dare you come here and claim to be the princess of Scotland and my cousin.' She waved her hand violently in front of Mary Elizabeth's face.

'I dare,' the princess answered. 'Because I was born with the right to dare. When all the forces of England and Scotland would have seen me dead at birth, I have risen above their powers and have come to claim my rights.'

'Your rights?' the queen glowered. Her heavily powered face was beginning to crumble, leaving behind the bulging veins of a very angry woman.

'Yes, my rights.' Mary Elizabeth matched the queen's glare. 'I am Princess Mary Elizabeth of Scotland, daughter of Queen Mary of Scotland, your cousin, remember her, the one you murdered!' There she had said it. The silence in the room was overwhelming. Eyes glued to each other, there was now a battle of wills at play.

'So, you claim.' The queen waved aside the princess's declaration. 'If that were so, if you were the princess who was born to Queen Mary at Loch Leven Castle, where have you been all these years? Can you explain that to me?'

'I was overseas,' Mary Elizabeth answered honestly. 'My mother gave me to a trusted servant just after I was born, to ensure I would not be disposed of, or worse, made a prisoner of the realm like she was. Then murdered. You cannot talk your way out of her execution, and you know it!'

The queen blanched at the mention of Queen Mary's execution. The princess knew she was being studied closely. She knew the queen would recognise the similarities she bore to the Scottish queen. Even though she never met her face to face, the princess knew that she had seen images of Queen Mary.

Holding the queen's gaze, the princess broke the silence, declaring 'I come bearing gifts.' She waved a hand and her faithful pageboy trotted up quickly. He had an elegant box in his hand, featuring the Stuart Crest: an argent pelican, winged and feeding her young in the nest. Underneath were engraved words, 'Virescti Vulnere Virtus,' which means, Courage grows strong at a wound. It was very appropriate, especially considering the contents inside the box.

Mary Elizabeth accepted the box and then handed it to the queen. Queen Elizabeth was reluctant to accept the so-called gift, but her curiosity won out. She read the inscription and pursing her lips, sent a glower look at the princess, then proceeded to open it, cautiously. She shrieked as the box and its contents were thrown aside, crashing at her feet. The blood-stained silk gloves of the beheaded Queen of Scots flew to the floor as the rosary beads broke from their binding and scattered across the floor.

'How dare you!' The queen spat out the words as she rose from her throne and pointed her finger. 'Arrest her. Arrest this pretender.'

'I dare you,' Mary Elizabeth responded as calmly as she could. 'I dare you to arrest me, like you did to my mother. I have an army in the thousands at the border awaiting my summons to move south. I dare you to arrest me, knowing that you have already done enough damage to your reputation by beheading my mother, your cousin an anointed queen.

Just then, a man stepped out from behind the throne. The princess had not noticed him there before. She flashed him her most brilliant smile. 'Robert Dudley, the Earl of Leicester. What a surprise to find you here, at your lover's beck and call, no less.'

There was a collective gasp from the lords and ladies who filled the royal chambers. No one dared voice their opinions of the queen's dalliance to her face. The queen was now livid, shaking her head, her red-headed fury in full force.

Turning to the queen, the unfazed Lord Dudley suggested 'Perhaps she could be your guest for a time.' With that Mary Elizabeth let out a full-bodied laugh.

'You cannot be serious. You think I would fall for that line? I suppose you mean to make me a guest of the tower. Guest or prisoner, it is all the same in your court. I could not list the number of royals who entered the tower as a 'guest' and left without their head. It does not matter, I will find my way out of whatever prison you chose.'

This time several chuckles were heard around the room, making the queen even more irritated. Trying to sound calm and polite, sitting back on her throne she said, 'maybe we should hear what it is the princess wants. She would not have risked her life just to give me her dead mother's gloves and rosary beads.'

'Tainted with her blood,' the princess added. 'She wore those gloves and carried those beads to her execution.' Noticing the fury on the queen's face she had to continue. 'Her blood splattered everywhere, not surprising as it took three strokes to severe her head. THREE STROKES! It should have only been one, but I'm guessing the executioner was supplied with a blunt sword. Horrific as it was to behead an innocent woman, a caring and compassionate queen. Probably praying for forgiveness for the one person she thought she could trust.' Then, lifting her hand, she pointed her finger at the queen and yelled, 'YOU! She respected you, she even named me after you and YOU KILLED HER!'

The room fell silent. The queen looked at the people of her court and then back to the princess. A total look of disbelief and anger flashed across her face.

'I never believed the rumours of a hidden princess and believe me I have searched the kingdom. You were overseas, you say, Ireland? The Irish are well known to take pleasure in harbouring someone with the potential to disrupt the power of the English throne. Just like my grandfather's pretenders did years ago.' The queen then forced her voice to sound calm and asked, 'Tell me what you want.'

'It is quite simple. When you die, and you will in the next twenty years or so, my brother, King James VI of Scotland, is your one and only heir. Give him the inheritance with the stipulation that the crown of Scotland goes to me so that Scotland remains independent for centuries to come.'

There was silence. This time it was the queen who started to laugh. 'You cannot be serious. This is ridiculous. How could you possibly know when I should die? You must be a witch. And we all know what happens to witches. 'Guards, seize her!'

Mary Elizabeth just shrugged. 'I tried to warn you.' She looked behind to see if Jamie and Lady Mary Catherine were still there. They were being surrounded by the queen's guards. Turning back to the queen, she added. 'When next we meet, I shall be at the head of a large army.'

'Not if I burn you first, take her away.' The queen demanded.

As they were led from the queen's chambers and turned the corner, out of sight, Jamie coughed. A signal. And just like that....

It seemed that they were still on the site of Greenwich Castle, but it was smaller and different somehow. People were walking around. Mary Elizabeth saw a huge dome overhead. The castle of Queen Elizabeth's time was long gone. In its place was the 21st century grandest piece of equipment, the gigantic telescope, in the Royal Observatory.

The security guards were baffled as the workers and visitors were starting to point at the people dressed in 16th century period costumes. One voice said, 'Wow talk about real life action.' Another said, 'Where did they come from?' They had to act quickly. Jamie whipped out his sword, Mary Elizabeth did the same. Before the security guards could reach them, they ran to the nearest door and headed down the corridor.

When they got outside, they hid behind some hedges and found themselves back in the 16th century with their horses waiting for them. As they started to gallop away, Mary Elizabeth pulled up next to one of the guards at the entrance and said, 'Tell her Majesty that I am not a witch but the next time she sees me it will be on the battlefield.'

With that she turned around and followed the others back to their camp, before making their departure to the north.

CHAPTER TWENTY-THREE

'What do you mean, she escaped?'

The queen stormed back and forth in front of the hearth in her private chambers.

'Where are the guards that escorted her from my presence?' She stood in front of the boy who stood before her, trembling. 'No one knows, your Majesty.' He spoke in a whisper.

'Speak up and look at me boy!' the queen screamed. She certainly had her father's temper.

He struggled to raise his head, tears slipping from his eyes and when he met her stare, he began trembling, even more. 'No one knows, your Majesty,' he repeated.

'How can it be that a palace full of my guards, and no one saw anything? Did they just disappear?'

'Apparently, that is exactly what happened,' the guard said. 'They vanished and then reappeared outside, mounting their horses. Before the princess galloped off, she spoke to me.' He tried to speak clearly although he did not want to repeat what the princess had said.

'Oh, for heavens sake boy, continue, I am not going to chop you to pieces.' The queen screamed.

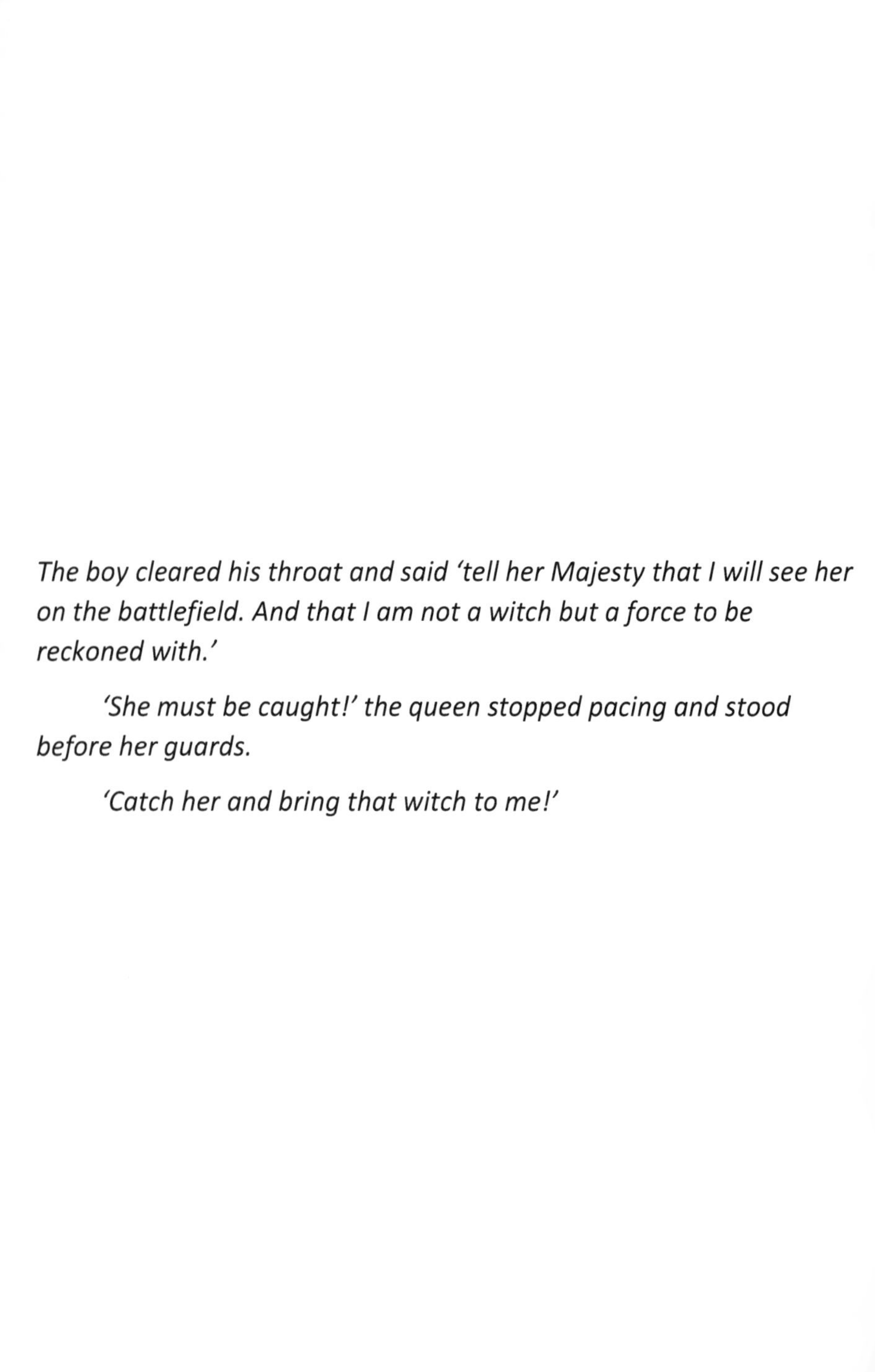

The boy cleared his throat and said 'tell her Majesty that I will see her on the battlefield. And that I am not a witch but a force to be reckoned with.'

'She must be caught!' the queen stopped pacing and stood before her guards.

'Catch her and bring that witch to me!'

CHAPTER TWENTY-FOUR

NORTH ENGLAND 1587

'There is a price on my head,' Mary Elizabeth announced as she met up with her grandmother the following day. 'What do you think, grandmother, do I continue on and visit my brother and then hide in Scotland for the next decade or do I meet her on the battlefield?'

'The queen thinks you are a witch. It might be best to hide out for a while. Visit your brother if you wish, but remember by the time you meet with him, he will already know about your meeting with the Queen of England and about your demands. He may want to imprison you himself.'

'Maybe I should just haunt her now and then to remind her, I told you so.'

'Be careful granddaughter. Time travel does not always work the way you want it to. I have known most of my life that I could jump through time and there have been occasions when it was helpful, like the day I died. I had been sick, for a while, and knew my only survival would be to get treatment in the future.

'So, time travel did and can help.'

'Yes, but not always. It did not help me save my sons, James and Robert.'

‘I did not know you had sons.’ Mary Elizabeth said. ‘I must have missed that in my history lessons.’

‘I had no warning,’ Gran continued. ‘I had no clue. I thought they were both strong.’

‘What happened?’

Gran dropped her head and shrugged her shoulders. ‘I do not know.’

‘I am so very sorry grandmother.’ Mary Elizabeth reached across and took hold of her grandmother’s hand. The old woman nodded and took a deep breath. ‘And when your grandfather was killed on the battlefield, I could have saved him,’ Gran continued. ‘My jaunts into the future at that time had not allowed me the time to read up on the 16th century. Had I done so, I might have been aware of the threat that lay ahead before my husband headed out to battle. So, you see Mary Elizabeth, time travel is not a crutch to use. Sometimes we just have to weather the storm.’

They rode in silence again. Mary Elizabeth broke the silence first. ‘Grandmother what do I do?’

‘First of all, do not go to your brother’s court.’ Her grandmother’s answer was firm. ‘I believe he already knows about your visit to Greenwich and he has a trap waiting for you. He wants to remain in the English queen’s good graces, at least until she dies and leaves him the throne.’

‘Do I just jump in time and meet him after Queen Elizabeth’s death?’ the princess asked.

‘Maybe you should do just that, but not yet,’ Gran advised. ‘First thing you do, hide out on one of the northern islands and wait. Time is your best ally. Your armies will rise again when you need them.’

The group came to a stop on a hill overlooking the land leading to Alnwick Castle. It looked empty. All the princess's supporters that had rallied there a few weeks ago where now gone.

'Where's my army?' the princess looked from one end of the castle to the next. Jamie galloped over to the women. 'It does not look good. It may be a trap. We might be better to continue north.' There discussion stopped when they noticed a lone rider approach.

'William,' Jamie called out. 'What's happening?'

'It's a trap, my lord. The army were given false information to meet you to the east and left a few days ago. The English have taken position in and around the castle. I know it looks deserted, but it is not.'

'Can we go around and make our way north?' Jamie asked. William shook his head. 'You would be best to go far west, then north. Unless you want to stay and fight.'

'What if we surround them and reversed the trap?' the princess asked, making sure she had a say in the matter. Jamie just shook his head. The Duke of Northumberland joined them 'how many English soldiers to you figure?' William shrugged, 'lots.'

'Well, we cannot just stand where they can see us,' Gran pointed out. 'Are they all inside the castle, or hidden around so they can trap us?'

'Mostly inside the castle.'

Jamie turned to the Duke. 'You know the castle better than anyone, Lord Thomas what would you suggest?'

'I suggest we weed out the scouts and surround the castle.' The Duke looked down to the home that had been taken from his inheritance with a look of determination. I just hope my family are safe within.'

'Is there a way to sneak inside and catch them unawares?' Mary Elizabeth asked. 'Perhaps after dark.' Lord Thomas nodded. 'But first we need to take out the scouts and get into position.' Turning to the Duke, Jamie asked, 'Your advice, Lord Thomas. Where would be best to set up our own blockade?'

'First, we wait until dark. Then we rescue my family, if they are still inside. Then we burn them out.'

Young Thomas pulled his horse beside his father. 'I must go in there,' he insisted. 'Not yet son. We must do as the princess commands. We must plan our strategy.' The Duke kept a firm hold on his son's arm.

'I will go,' the princess announced. 'It is me they want. They would not dare harm me, the queen wants me alive so she can watch me burn at the stake, something that will never happen. Jamie and Thomas can come and rescue me while the army outside ignite the castle.

'Are you sure you want to do that?' Gran asked. 'It seems a bit drastic, after all, this is your life, the welfare of Scotland and the Duke of Northumberland's family home.'

'Not anymore,' the duke answered. Queen Elizabeth made sure of that. I will stake my claim north of the border and fight for the princess, who, I am sure will honour her valiant warriors.'

Mary Elizabeth beamed at Thomas, the man that should have inherited this castle and the title that went with it. The young man could not help but wink at the princess, which made her blush. 'I will indeed, my lord. I will find you a suitable Scottish title and a castle befitting a true warrior.'

The Duke bowed his head before turning to Jamie. 'Let us make haste before we our noticed.'

They turned their horses around and led the princess's small army back into the forest.

Nightfall would come and with it, the destruction of a noble edifice. And all because the Queen of England wanted Princess Mary Elizabeth dead, just like her mother.

CHAPTER TWENTY-FIVE

NORTH OF THE SCOTTISH BORDER

LATE SUMMER 1587

The image of the noble Alnwick Castle, riddled with flames, burning from the inside out, haunted the princess's sleep. It had been over a week but every night it haunted her dreams.

As their group moved even further north, they crossed the border into Scotland and moved as far west of Edinburgh as they could, trying to avoid King James and his allies.

Over the last week the princess had been forced to admit that King James would not be of any assistance to her cause.

The castle, gutted by the ravaging flames, was something she could not erase from her memory. She realised that all battles left scars, but this one felt more horrifying, perhaps by the fact that she, Lord Northumberland and his family almost perished in the raging inferno.

The plan had gone well though. Lord Northumberland had successfully captured Sir Thomas Cecil, the queen's man, and several key players from the queen's court. They would serve as good hostages to use on the bargaining table.

Mary Elizabeth took pleasure in, once again, sending a message to her cousin, a message that she, Princess Mary Elizabeth of Scotland, would not and could not be defeated.

Even after all that, the scar of Alnwick was too much to bear. There was nothing left. Just a shell.

CHAPTER TWENTY-SIX

BOTHWELL CASTLE 1588

The journey north was way too long. Mary Elizabeth loved horses, but day after day in the saddle was becoming extremely hard on her back. She made her group stop briefly at Bothwell Castle. The 13th century castle with its circular tower, proudly stood, keeping guard between the castle and the waters of the Clyde.

Jamie investigated and was satisfied that all was clear, except for a small handful of staff, so he agreed to accompany the princess. She wanted to search for her father's hidden cache, although she wasn't sure if it was here or at one of the other castles that he had mentioned on her frequent visits to his prison cell.

They made their way to the castle gates as if they were on a Royal Progress.

'Who goes there?' the question came from behind the enclosure.

'Princess Mary Elizabeth of Scotland,' Jamie answered in response. 'Daughter of the late Queen Mary of Scotland and her husband, James Hepburn, fourth Earl of Bothwell. She is on tour of Scotland visiting her late father's estates.

The voice called out again. 'We have received no word from the current Lord Bothwell. On whose authority do I allow your admittance?'

'On the authority of the Princess Mary Elizabeth of Scotland and her loyal followers,' James replied.

'You may enter, but only for a brief visit.' The guard, looking at the princess, gave a bow. 'You must understand, Princess, these are difficult times and one can never be too sure who to trust. In another time and place, I would instantly offer you my allegiance, but if the current King, your brother, ever heard, I would most probably lose my head.'

'I understand, sir. It is very kind of you to allow us inside for a brief visit. I just want to spend a few moments, so I can get a feel of the father I never had the opportunity to meet. Did you know my father, sir?' She gave him a warm smile.

'Aye, I did, Princess. I was just a lad at the time, but I had the honour of knowing him. He was kind to me. A good man. Come inside out of the cold. You may sit in his private study and look at some of his books and other treasures.'

The soldier led Mary Elizabeth through the hall and down a corridor to a large elaborately carved panel door that led into a spacious room, covered wall-to-wall with bookshelves full of books. Jamie came up behind them. 'Perhaps the princess could have sometime alone while she studies her father's treasures?' The soldier nodded and gave the princess a short bow, before leaving the room.

She turned around in a circle, taking everything in. For a 16th century Scottish Lord, her father certainly had a large collection of books, presumably all hand printed. It was truly remarkable, considering the printing press had only been developed in the last century or so and books were still, at this point, considered something of a rarity, so to see a room full of them was amazing.

She walked over to the shelf closest to her and inspected the spines. 'Pure leather. These are all in pristine condition.' She noted. 'Shakespeare's *Macbeth*.' Mary Elizabeth cautiously opened the top page and let out a gasp. 'It's autographed by the man himself! My father must have met him. But how? It cannot be.' She looked over her shoulder at Jamie standing at the desk in the corner. He stopped searching and looked up at her.

'What do you mean, it cannot be? Why not?'

'Because, Jamie.' The princess shook her head and continued to study the pages in front of her, 'this is 1588, *Macbeth* was first published in 1606, and Shakespeare's plays were not published until after his death.'

Jamie just shrugged. 'Perhaps the playwright was a time traveller.'

'Do you think so?'

Jamie shrugged again. 'Not worth thinking about now. We have little time to search this room. Keep it, if you must. Was it personally autographed to your father?'

'Yes,' she replied. 'It reads: *To James Hepburn, an honourable Lord of the North, whose assistance on this production I greatly appreciate.* Shakespeare must have consulted with my father while he was writing this. I had not realised my father was a passionate Scottish historian. This is amazing!'

'Slip it into the bag you always carry along with your mother's treasure box.' Mary Elizabeth nodded and did as he suggested.

'In here, my lords,' the soldier's voice boomed from the entry hall.

The princess gasped. 'Someone comes.'

'Behind the desk.' Jamie motioned quickly.

'Hide and stay just long enough to see what threat these lords present.' 'You mean if they are in fact, lords?' Mary Elizabeth ran behind the desk just as the door burst open and they heard heavy footsteps marching forward.

'Where are they?' the voice was English, almost too English, to be from this era. 'You said they were here. What have you done with them? Where have you hidden them?'

'They were just here.' The soldier gasped as if something had tightened around his throat, before he fell to the ground.

'Search the castle.' That was the English voice again. 'They could not have gone far. Unless they jumped time again.' Another English voice.

'If they have, we shall be right behind them. We have got to capture the princess before she makes further contact with the people of this era and totally disrupts the timeline. Go. I will look here.'

The footsteps came closer. 'I know you are in here, Princess, if that is what you wish to be called. Time to come out and face reality. The future needs you back in your own time. Come on, Princess, don't be difficult.

Jamie moved closer and held her hand. She nodded in understanding. Just as the footsteps stopped on the other side of the desk, the two made their jump into the future. They found themselves in Gran's house in Dublin, just before the escape that had left the house in a rubble of bricks. They barely heard the 'I'm right behind you,' when they jumped again back in time, as the house exploded with their pursuant inside.'

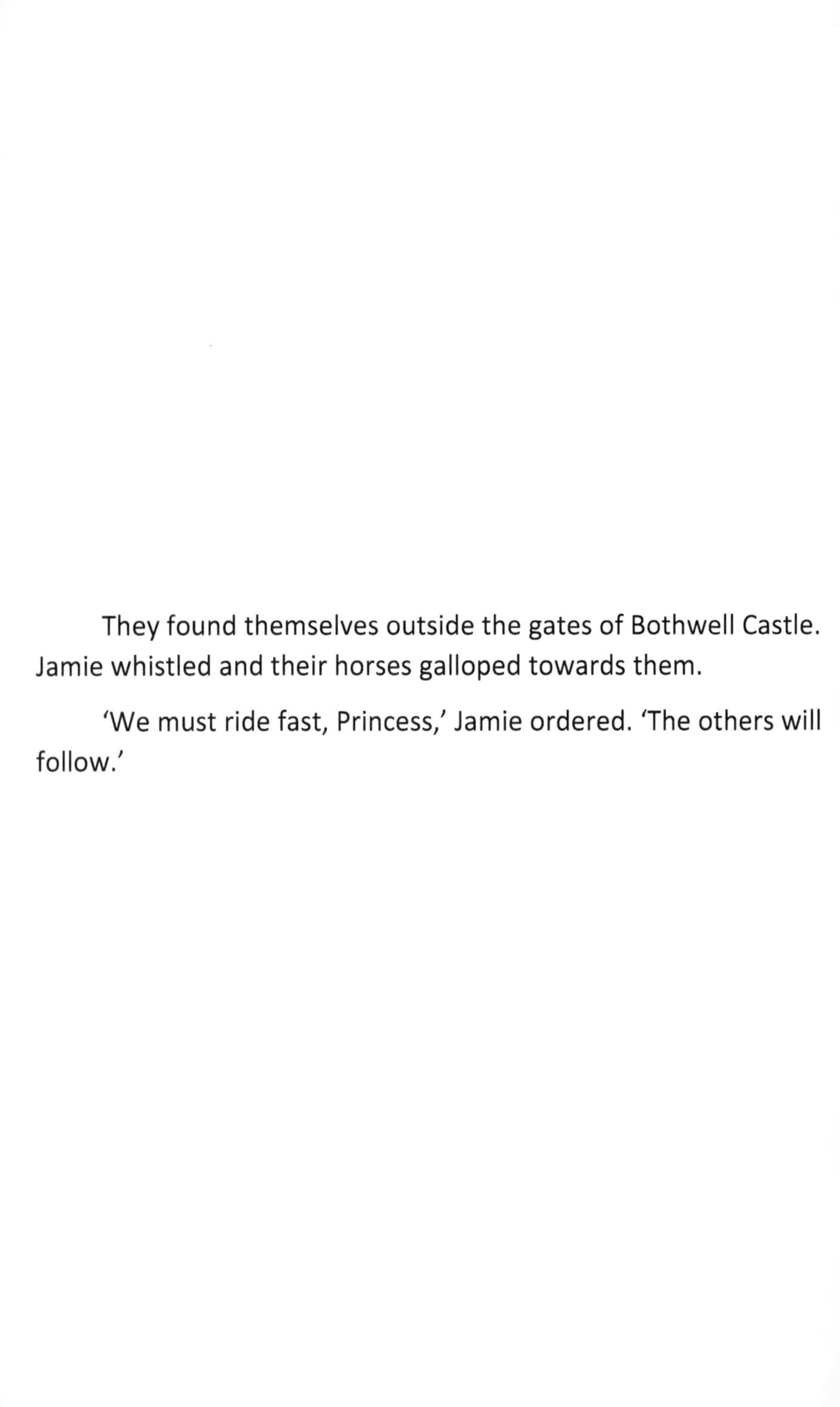

They found themselves outside the gates of Bothwell Castle. Jamie whistled and their horses galloped towards them.

'We must ride fast, Princess,' Jamie ordered. 'The others will follow.'

CHAPTER TWENTY-SEVEN

LINLITHGOW CASTLE

LATE SUMMER 1588

'A message from the Queen of England, Your Majesty, in relation to your sister.'

'I have no sister,' James stated, pacing the floor of his private chambers restlessly. 'My mother would have told me, would she not? All those letters, all those years of letters from my mother and no mention of a sister.'

He came to a stop at the window, without turning, he waved dismissively.

'Read the queen's missive,' the king commanded.

The messenger handed the letter to the king's lover, George, Captain of the King's Guard.

'My dear Cousin, the pretender who claims to be your sister is a witch. Capture her and have her executed as befitting her status in the black arts. Until she is dead, there will be no official acknowledgement of you becoming my rightful heir.'

'No!' King James shouted. 'She cannot do this to me. I am her only legitimate heir. What does she think she is going to do?

Suddenly give birth to a child to take the throne? She is how old now? Fifty? Sixty?'

'We must do what she says, Your Majesty,' George pointed out. 'This so-called princess is also a threat to your throne.'

'I know, I know.' 'Do you know where she is?'

'She is in Scotland. Probably way up north.'

'Well, she can stay up there, perhaps she will freeze to death.' King James walked back to the window and watched the rain. 'I once thought I would like to have a sister. Leave me.'

As the door closed, the king stood alone in his chamber.

'I am touched,' a woman's voice startled the king from his gaze.

'Who's there and who let you into my private chambers,' he demanded.

'I let myself in, brother.' She dipped a curtsy and smiled as she stood up. Taking a step closer, she said, 'I have always wanted a brother. Now we both have what we wanted.'

'You are not who you say you are!' King James bellowed.

'Oh, but I am,' the princess said sweetly.

'What kind of Witch are you?'

'I am not a witch. I am a princess and I am your sister. Or should I say, your half-sister, since we did not share the same father.'

'You claim to be my mother's daughter and the daughter of her lover, Lord Bothwell.' The king started to pace again.

'They may have been lovers, but they were also legally married,' Mary Elizabeth insisted. 'Do you want to argue about my ancestry, or shall we discuss what is best for this kingdom? What is best for Scotland.'

'I am the King of Scotland. And when Queen Elizabeth dies, I shall also be the King of England and Ireland. That is my birth-right.'

'Your right by birth *includes a responsibility, brother. The English have never liked the Scottish, and under a combined rule they will quickly overrun Scotland, just as they have done in Ireland for generations. Take* England's *throne and rule England. Leave Scotland to me,' Mary* Elizabeth *stated bluntly.*

A knock on the door interrupted their argument. King James looked towards the chamber door.

'Is everything all right in there, Your Majesty?' George called through the door.

'All is well,' the king replied. He turned back to his sister, but she had vanished.

CHAPTER TWENTY-EIGHT

RICHMOND PALACE

24TH MARCH 1603

'What do you want?' the voice said is a whisper. The figures head, which was all that could be seen above the coverings in the canopied bed was bald. The chest barely rising, indicating that there was some life left, but not much.

Mary Elizabeth was startled by the voice. She had not expected to converse with Elizabeth, not in this state, and not so near the end of her life. The Queen of England was dying, and she was alone. It was a tragic way to go, isolated and frightened by what lay ahead on the other side.

The princess knelt-down beside the bed and took the queen's hand. It felt cold, but delicate. This was not the hand of the all-powerful Queen of England, the woman who only had to raise her hand to have others bow to her or quiver with fear. She had once pointed that very hand, that Mary Elizabeth now held, accusingly at her, calling her a witch. And had accepted the gift with the same hand, the gift Mary Elizabeth had given her, in front of her entire court, her mother's rosary beads and blood-stained gloves, that Mary Queen of Scotland had worn to her execution.

Maybe it was better to die young and become a legend, than to wither away like this. 'Where is everyone?' Mary Elizabeth asked.

'Where are your ladies? The priest? Should they not be here with you?'

'To do what, watch me die?' the queen let out a small cough. 'I am dying. It is my time. I would rather be alone.'

The princess shook her head. She had known this would be the day the Queen of England died. Mary Elizabeth remembered her studies in history, the studies she had done in the 21st century. She also remembered reading about how the queen had worn lead-infested make-up, that had made her sick for a long time before killing her. She looked at the queen. 'It must be the powder you have used for all these years. It has poisoned your body,' Mary Elizabeth whispered.

A glimmer of a smile appeared on the queen's face, her eyes lifted slightly to look at the princess. 'That powder made me look so young and beautiful. I was a beautiful queen, was I not?'

'Aye,' Mary Elizabeth replied and smiled, trying to look compassionate for the woman who had taken so much from her. The Queen of England had stolen her mother and her birth-right, and now she was the one who lay in her bed helpless. But there was no one here but herself: The Queen of England and the Princess of Scotland, once-accused of being a witch and hunted for years and all by this sad figure lying on the bed.

Mary Elizabeth knew the last few years had been difficult. In fact, the queen's problems could be traced back to that fateful day when her orders were carried out, and the Queen of Scotland was executed for treason, a treason which she did not commit. Then there was the Spanish Armada, and the years of famine that followed had not helped. The people blamed all this on Queen Elizabeth.

Sensing the princess's thoughts, the queen gave a little nod. 'They will forget me and rejoice with their new king, your brother.'

Noticing the shocked looked on the princess's face, she added, 'Yes. I am beginning to accept your claim. You are your mother's daughter in so many ways. You are the Princess of Scotland and my cousin.'

'If only you had accepted me sooner,' the princess replied sadly. 'And when James comes to accept his crown, what then? What will happen to Scotland?'

The queen gently squeezed Mary Elizabeth's hand. 'I am sure you will manage. You must make things right for your country. I am sure you will make a great queen, as I did once. I have ruled my country for forty-five years and I know you will too. After all, we are cousins. It is in our blood.

Mary Elizabeth stayed with the queen until drew her last breath. No one should die alone.

'You ruled well, dear cousin and that is how history will remember you.' Mary Elizabeth got up from beside the queen's bed and made her way to the door. Opening it, she spoke in a clear voice, so to be heard. 'The Queen of England, Elizabeth I, last of the Tudor line is dead. Long live King James VI of Scotland, soon to be King James I of England and Ireland. And long live Queen Mary Elizabeth of Scotland!'

As the figures in the hallway jumped to attention and repeated Mary Elizabeth's accolades, the soon to be Queen of Scotland vanished.

CHAPTER TWENTY-NINE

KIRKWALL CASTLE

ORKNEY ISLANDS 1603

Mary Elizabeth was feeling restless and lonely. Stuck within the walls of the castle day in, day out. Was this rain ever going to stop. And of course, she kept reliving the visit with her cousin on her last night. It was sad to see such a great queen die alone.

Jamie had insisted they stay in the Orkney Islands as a place of refuge until the crown was passed onto King James. The islands were far north and inaccessible, especially in this stormy weather, so they would serve as a safe-haven until she raised her army and made her way south again.

Gran and Lady Mary Catherine had returned to Dublin in the future to wait, but they promised they would return in time to see Mary Elizabeth claim the Scottish throne. Neither of them wanted to age too quickly in the past while they waited.

During this time, Mary Elizabeth had made the occasional jump to the future, more to ease her mind from boredom, while she was isolated. She had even made a few jumps back in time, when her parents were still alive.

She followed Lord Bothwell, hoping to find the hiding place of his treasure, the one he claimed would help her finance her campaign. She believed she now knew where to look and when she began to make her way south to claim her throne, she would retrieve it then. But even with the occasional jumps through time, the days and nights were still very long and lonely.

Lady Jane, her mother's maid, whom the princess had met the night before her mother's execution had decided to stay with the princess, and over the years Mary Elizabeth and Lady Jane had become quite close. She felt she could trust Jane, which was rare. But she was also blessed to have a large and lively court with attendants that had served in her mother's court, including the Earl of Northumberland's family. As her court grew, she knew she was making her presence felt. A presence that was threatening to both Queen Elizabeth and King James.

That thought always made her smile. Her cause was making an impact on the entire United Kingdom, not that it was known as the United Kingdom in the 16th and 17th century. But if King James succeeded in uniting Scotland to England and Ireland under the one crown, and after all his promises to maintain individual governments in Scotland and Ireland, then the Brexit of the 21st century had the potential of blowing all of Europe off balance as Scotland challenged the powers to regain its independence.

A knock on the door startled the princess from her thoughts and Lady Jane entered. 'There is a messenger in the grand hall,' she announced. 'Any idea what news?' the princess asked. 'I could not hear all of the conversation between the Earl and your Jamie,' Lady Jane said with a mischievous smile. 'Jamie? He is here?' Mary Elizabeth could not help but blush.

'Aye, he is.' Jane replied, perfecting the princess's hair. 'He arrived with the messenger. It appears your brother is on his way south to claim his new crown. The Queen of England is dead. Long live the King. And long live the new Queen of Scotland.'

‘Finally!’ Mary Elizabeth lifted her head high and made her way out of her chambers.

As she entered the grand hall, the guard at the door made the announcement. ‘Her Majesty Queen Mary Elizabeth of Scotland.’ Mary Elizabeth nearly stumbled hearing his words. She was not expecting the elevation so soon. She walked slowly towards the gathering of people at the far end of the room, as she did everyone bowed.

‘Jamie,’ She held out her hand. He was on bended knee with his head bowed. ‘Your Majesty.’ As Mary Elizabeth glanced behind Jamie, she noticed two women seated by the fire.

‘Grandmother. Lady Mary Catherine!’ She moved directly towards them and planted a kiss on each of their cheeks.

The two women were now looking their age, although she was unsure of what that was. Gran looked particularly old looking. Concern etched across her brow. She was about to speak but noticed a broad smile appearing on Gran’s face. ‘What brings you all here?’ the princess asked, looking a little confused.

Clearing his throat, Jamie replied, ‘News has brought us all her, my Queen.’

‘Queen?’ the princess asked.

Jamie then proceeded. He announced for all to hear, ‘On the 24th of March, in the year of our Lord 1603, Queen Elizabeth the first of England and Ireland died. On receiving the news of her death, King James VI of Scotland assembled his army and headed south to claim the throne of England, Ireland and Scotland. The people of Scotland have no desire to be pawns to the King of England. Although King James has assured us that Scotland will maintain their own parliament and laws, he has assigned English lords to oversee the governance of Scotland. The people of Scotland are raising armies as we speak to proclaim the Princess Mary Elizabeth, daughter of Mary Queen of Scots and sister to King James I of England, Ireland and Scotland, to be the one true monarch to lead Scotland. I have been sent here as the spokesperson of the Scottish Council of Lords to ask the Princess Mary Elizabeth if she will accept the crown of Scotland. Let us keep our country free now and forever.'

Before Mary Elizabeth could answer, a loud cheer erupted, with voices calling out 'Long live Mary Elizabeth of Scotland. Long live the Queen.'

When the cheering had died down, the new Queen of Scotland began greeting her countrymen and women.

'People of Scotland,' she said in a clear and happy voice. 'I accept the crown and the title. I promise to keep our land safe from English tyranny and unwanted dominance from any foreign nation. We are strong and free.'

The grand hall of Kirkwall Castle erupted in cheers.

CHAPTER THIRTY

EDINBURGH CASTLE

JULY 1603

Mary Elizabeth sat tall on her white filly. She was excited to be making this historic march. She wore the traditional plaid of the Royal Stuart clan as a tartan sash across her shoulders held in place with the brooch that had been given to her back in Kinross, when she made her first journey back in time. The striking red matched the red velvet lining of the Royal Scottish crown that she wore on her head.

Jamie had jumped across the time vortex to retrieve the Scottish Crown the one King James had locked away in the Tower of London. He had secured the crown at great risk, but with his excellent time travel skills the crown was now back where it belonged – in Scotland and now on the head of the new Scottish monarch.

Wearing the crown now as Scotland's anointed Queen, Mary Elizabeth rode with pride through Edinburgh. The procession along the Royal Mile from Holyrood Palace to Edinburgh Castle, was the new queen's opportunity to address her people. After the coronation in Scone, Gran and Lady Mary Catherine had both passed away within days of each other. She missed her grandmother terribly, but she knew that both her mother and grandmother were watching her always. She also knew that she would see her grandmother again, as she had told her that she had jumped from the 20th century to her future as Queen of Scotland in the 17th century. She still had Jamie by her side.

The Scottish people had come out to show their support and affection. 'Long live Queen Mary Elizabeth of Scotland. Long live the Queen.' The chants and well wishes carried her along as she nodded and waved in recognition of her people.

When they approached the castle gates, they made their way through another large gathering at the far end of the courtyard. Mary Elizabeth reined in her horse and turned to face her people.

'My good Scottish people,' she said in a commanding voice. 'We are at a crossroads in our history, one that requires our strength and perseverance. I had a dream that our country was united with England and Ireland and the generations of fighting with our English neighbours had gone against us. In this dream, generations of proud Scottish people were wiped out as the English overran our country, destroying our lands and our people.' She paused briefly to allow her words sink in. 'I had a dream that this land we are so proud to call our own, became the scourge that sent our people away to find new homes in far away countries. It was not a nice dream. I never want any of that happening to our country or our people.'

'I do have a dream, my good Scottish people, of a more promising future. In this dream, Scotland remains free, strong and safe for all our people. In this dream we stand up for our independence and we keep our country strong and free, for now and forever.'

The crowd began chanting 'now and forever.'

'For now, and Forever! Long live the queen!'

To which the new queen responded, 'Long live Scotland, strong and free!'

CHAPTER THIRTY-ONE

TOWER OF LONDON

25TH JULY 1603

'I do not understand how she managed to find her way south to Edinburgh. We had everywhere well-guarded.' King James paced the floor in his coronation robes.

'The guards were Scottish, your Majesty.' George, the Captain of the King's Guards nervously responded. 'They believe in her cause and were easily coerced into joining her army.

'And I hear she has crowned herself Queen Mary Elizabeth of Scotland? How dare she.'

'She insists, your Majesty. She insists that you also recognise her claim and allow the Scottish people to remain free. She was crowned in Scone, kneeling on the Stone of Destiny (Scotland's coronation stone). Then she marched through the streets of Edinburgh wearing the Royal Crown of Scotland.'

'The one I wore when I rode to London?' the king continued to pace. 'How did it end up back in Scotland? I thought it was locked in the Tower with England's Crown Jewels.'

'We are investigating that, your Majesty.'

The King held his hands against his forehead, in the hope of wiping out all the images of her. He was supposed to rule three countries. And now, some wee girl, claiming to be his sister had taken away one of his crowns. All because she believed in the freedom and independence of Scotland. 'Now and forever.' The king repeated the words he knew his sister had said for all the Scottish people.

'Does she not know that I have already promised the Scottish people their own governing body?'

'It does not matter, your Majesty,' George replied. 'She claims that your position of power will only be effective during your lifetime, and that you cannot guarantee what happens to the Scottish people at the hands of the English, in generations to come.'

'Neither can she,' the king argued.

'She is claiming that she can, your Majesty.'

'This is the news that I must hear on the day I am to be crowned King James I of England, Ireland and Scotland! Scotland is my birth-right, as well as England and Ireland. I will not allow that little lass take it all from me.'

'She does not want the crowns of England and Ireland, your Majesty, just Scotland.'

'Get out!'

'Yes, your Majesty.'

The door closed and the King stood alone in his chamber, trying to calm down. He had planned for this day all his life. How could it be taken from him so easily? And by no other than his sister?

'You have your father's temper, I see,' Mary Elizabeth stepped out from the shadows at the other end of the King's chamber. 'It does not suit you, then again, it did not suit Henry Darnley either. Perhaps his feeble-minded efforts to take control of our mother's court were

the beginning of his downfall. And here you are, just like him, plotting to keep it all for yourself. But you cannot James!'

'King James to you,' King James starred at the woman walking towards him.

'Just like your father,' she was shaking her head and tutting with disappointment at her brother's words.

'How would you know? He died before you were born.'

'Oh, you would be surprised by what I know. And I will address you as James. You are my brother. Besides, I am of equal rank to you now that I am the anointed Queen of Scotland.'

'I will have you executed,' James yelled back.

'You mean executed, like our mother was. I never could figure out why, when you came of age and took over the role of King of Scotland, you did not demand the safe release of our mother.'

'That is none of your concern. It was all political.'

'Oh yes, I can see that! You wanted to keep yourself in Elizabeth's good graces so that she would name you her heir. You did not want our mother returning to Scotland and raise an army to defend her claim to your throne. With mother out of the way, you had nothing to fear. You believed England and Ireland would be yours once the Queen of England had died. And you also believed that the Scottish people would not mind you taking the throne of their generations-old enemy. James, you should know your history better than that. The Scottish people do not want to be aligned with England.'

'Guards! Guards!' the king began to yell.

'You will recognise me as Queen of Scotland, James.' The voice faded away. 'The Scottish people will maintain their independence. 'Now and forever.'

'Guards!'

The King's guards burst into his chamber.

'Arrest her.' He pointed towards the window, his hand shaking from temper.

'Who? Your Majesty?' One of the guards asked.

Mary Elizabeth had vanished.

CHAPTER THIRTY-TWO

HOLYROOD HOUSE

1603

Jamie and the queen sat alone in her chambers moments before they had to leave for battle against King James.

'It would be my greatest wish, my dream come true,' Jamie continued, knowing that he could speak openly with the queen when they were alone like this. It was the only time they could speak like equals and call each other by their given names instead of addressing each other by their rank.

'And for the good of Scotland, Mary Elizabeth, Queen of Scotland and queen of my heart, I would love to be your husband.'

'Oh Jamie. I am most happy.' Mary Elizabeth threw her arms around him. She had finally taken a leap of faith and made her feelings known. After all this time together, she had asked him to be her partner in marriage, to father her children and heirs as well as helping her rule Scotland.

They both promised to make the official announcement when they returned from battle.

Before leaving to meet up with the queen's army, Jamie stopped at the chamber door and traced his finger down Mary Elizabeth's face. He gently lifted her chin and placed a lingering kiss on her lips.

'And our love will always be now and forever'.

CHAPTER THIRTY-THREE

HADRIAN'S WALL

OCTOBER 1603

The sun had not fully risen, but Mary Elizabeth knew her men were armed and ready. The order had gone out the night before, to claim the peak of the wall for miles around them. She chose Hadrian's wall because of its significant length. It made a good line of defence, as well as a defining border. She was not going to allow 17th century warfare dictate how they would fight this battle.

She was not going to line her men up to be picked off one by one by the enemy. Her plan was to fight from all sides. Her men were scattered all over the countryside. They had, quite literally, surrounded the King of England and his army. He and his troops had nowhere to run, and nowhere to hide. Only the Scots would be victorious today.

Once she settled in the saddle, Mary Elizabeth nudged her horse forward, moving gracefully through the camp. Cheers erupted as she made her progress. 'Long live Queen Mary Elizabeth of Scotland. Long live the Queen. Scotland the free, now and forever!'

The queen raised her hand to acknowledge the greetings and smiled warmly to her men. They were risking so much to stand with her on this day. If they were not successful, they would prob lose more than their lives. Their families would lose their homes.

That is, if the English won. Mary Elizabeth, Queen of Scotland was determined not to let that happen. She would fight to the death herself if need be, but she knew that would also be a futile exercise, as without her as their queen, the Scottish people could not possibly claim their independence. At least not now, in the 17th century.

'For Scotland!' she called out as she drew her sword. 'Now and Forever!'

'For Scotland. Now and Forever!' the soldiers marched beside her, continuing their chants as they approached the old wall. As the sun rose over the horizon, the shadows of men lined the top of the wall. They were unstoppable, strong and ready to follow her to victory.

Cheers echoed along the wall as the queen and her men looked down on the English camp. Mary Elizabeth, having studied history extensively, knew the history of warfare. Her plan was blunt and to the point. Her men, the ones surrounding the camp, had started to make their move. She could see their figures descending upon the unsuspecting English army. The queen sat on her horse and watched with pride and gratitude.

As she watched, she could smell the smoke of the many fires that burned along their side of the wall, ready to ignite the powder kegs. Jamie had seen to the improvements of the powerful cannons. He had overseen the Scottish blacksmiths in the manufacture of dozens of cannons, some for this battle and others to protect important castles within Scotland itself.

It had been a challenge to mount the cannon effectively along the wall, but the result was a hidden force from the enemy, one that would inflict considerable damage.

As she surveyed the east, knowing that Jamie was leading the force from that direction, she recognised his horse, draped with the Royal Stuart colours. Her heart went out to him.

The English camp began rustling into action. It was a scene of complete chaos which intensified as the Scottish force reached the camp and started attacking. The battle was almost over before it had begun. Jamie led his contingent directly to the King's tent and pulled his horse up facing the entry. His voice could be heard across the moors as he called out with purpose and power, 'My Lord, King James I of England, we have you surrounded, and we request that you come with us.'

There was movement from the royal tent. The Scottish forces next to the queen yelled enthusiastically as they saw the king come out from his tent. That's when it happened. A lone English archer, one unnoticed by the Scottish invaders, lifted his bow and took aim. He let the arrow fly and hit its mark.

'NO!' the queen screamed. She watched in horror as her beloved Jamie toppled lifeless from his horse.

'NO!'

She sat frozen on her horse, incapable of moving. She was startled out of her complacency by the yelling of the captain in command of her soldiers on the wall.

'Over there,' he yelled, pointing towards the horizon. The English banner flew high, blowing in the breeze as a mounted force approached the camp from the west. 'Rally around the queen, protect her at all cost.'

The English had not fallen for the ambush. It did not matter. Mary Elizabeth had expected as much. Jamie had argued late into the night, pointing out that they needed a reserve army, one that was unseen by the enemy, in case another force appeared to rally in defence of the captured king. Jamie had been right again. What was she going to do in the future, now that the man that had always been by her side, the one with all the right answers, her love, was no longer there? But she knew that she would see him again in the future. Her future, his past.

She pulled on the reins of her horse and faced her scout. Bill Douglas, now Sir William Douglas as she had knighted him as soon as she was crowned queen. He had remained loyal and reliable all these years, since the first time she met him in the cottage near Fotheringhay. 'GO. NOW.'

Jamie had made it clear to Sir William what had to be done if they were faced with this scenario. With the queen's command, Sir William nodded before moving away from the force that guarded the hill. The English were quickly approaching. Mary Elizabeth could only imagine the smirk on her brother's face. He was so sure of himself. What he didn't realise was that so was she.

The queen raised her sword high and gave the rallying cry. 'Scotland the free, now and forever.'

Not waiting for arguments to hold her back, she led the charge down the slope towards the approaching cavalry. She would lead her people to victory, even if she were to suffer a few cuts and bruises in the process. What kind of a ruler sat back and let others do the dangerous jobs?

Her protectors were shocked by the queen's sudden charge, but they were left with little choice. With the queen's strong presence leading them forward, how could they possibly fail. She heard her captain give the orders to fire the cannons. She knew how to fight; no one could argue that. As she charged in, slashing her sword left and right, she managed to unmount several English soldiers and wound others. Their momentum slowed, and the English kept coming. Their number far exceeded the Scottish.

Just as the English captain grabbed the reins of the queen's horse and took her sword, the battle cry of the Scottish shattered the English presumption of victory. Sir William led the charge of her reserve troops. Although she was a little startled at the audacity of the English captain, Mary Elizabeth quickly regained her composure. Before the captain could react, the queen took back her sword and instantly gave it a strong swing. The captain dropped his sword as the queen grazed his wrist with unexpected force. Before he could retaliate, the queen held the point of her sword to his neck.

'George Gordon, Captain of the King's Guard and the King's heart. Too bad you will not see your lover again, as I will not be seeing mine.' With that, she slashed the sword across his neck, shock and disbelief appeared on the victim's face before he slumped forward in the saddle.

'Take me to your King.' She reached over to make sure her victim was safely saddled on his mount. 'Perhaps you cannot take me now, so I shall take you. I do believe victory is ours.'

The rest of the battle was over shortly after. The queen guided what was left of the captain, slumped over his horse toward the English camp. The King remained standing by his tent, his guards on their knees with Scottish swords at their necks. He looked up as the queen came closer. Eyeing the horse beside her that carried his dead lover, the king looked heartbroken, and it did not go unnoticed by the queen.

'You killed James Stuart, Earl of Moray. I have had the pleasure of taking the life of George Gordon.' Then in a whisper so only the king could hear she said, 'the one you hold most dear.'

The King's face reddened with anger, but he was in no position to fight back. 'What do you want?' he snarled.

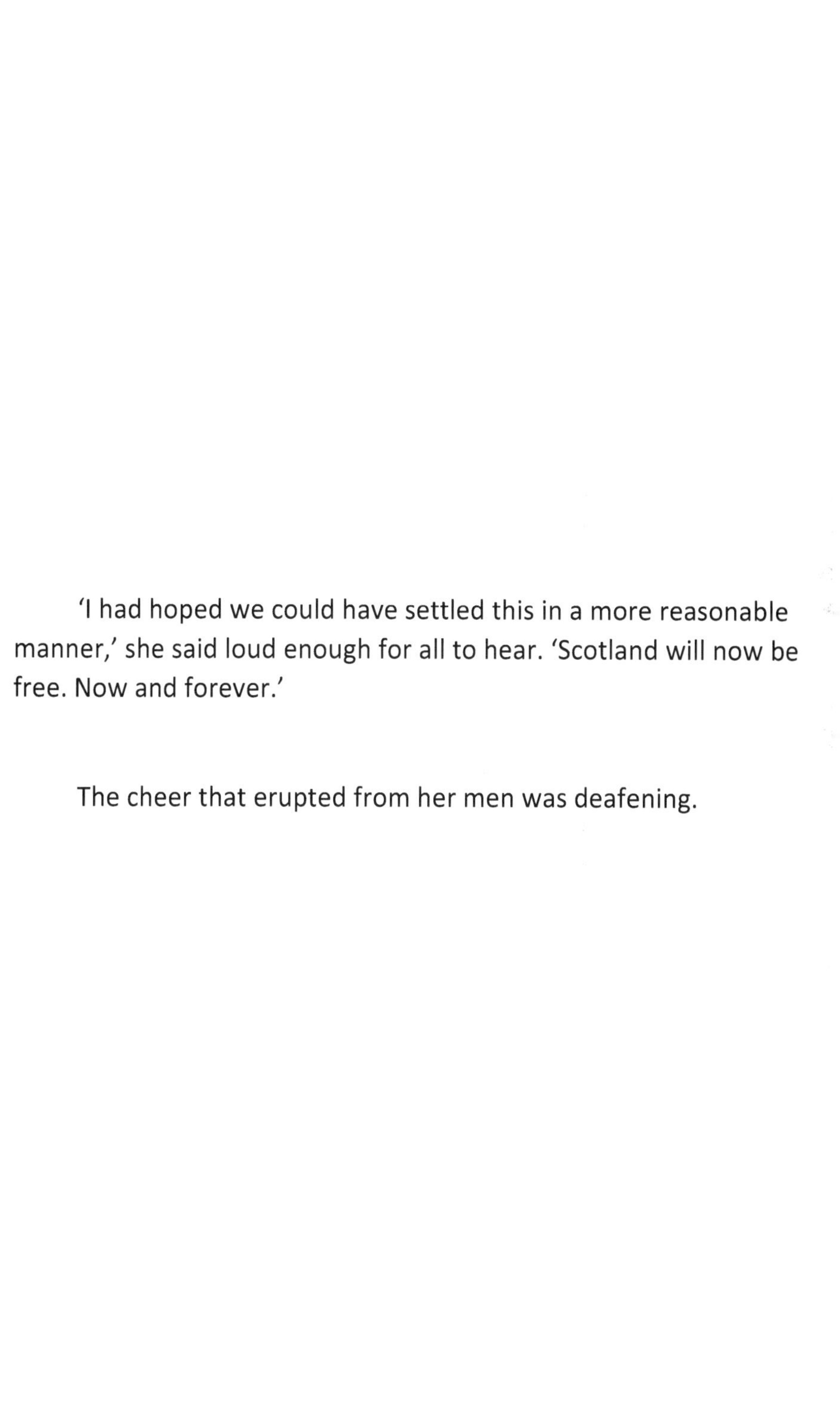

'I had hoped we could have settled this in a more reasonable manner,' she said loud enough for all to hear. 'Scotland will now be free. Now and forever.'

The cheer that erupted from her men was deafening.

CHAPTER THIRTY-FIVE

HOLYROOD HOUSE

30TH MARCH 1649

The queen sighed deeply as she sat back in her chair by the fire. Sitting still had never been easy for her. Now that the years had crept up on her and her joints showed signs of arthritis, as well as aging, she still found it annoying, not being able to move as quick. Where had all the years gone?

She pulled the small side table closer so she could continue her writing. She had decided it was time to record her memories in a journal before it was too late. Time was short, for her at least. It was always about time. The time now and the time in the future.

She knew Gran, Lady Mary Catherine and Jamie had all recorded theirs. She had read all their stories. One thing she did know, was her final days were coming to an end. All three of their journals had an entry dated 30th March 1649, today, and each of them stated that they had made their jump in time to say good-bye to Queen Mary Elizabeth of Scotland. It was evident then, that she only had a few hours left to live.

She had a lot that she wanted to do in that time, so many things to write, so many things to tell her family. There was a lot of things she needed to write down for future time travellers. She knew there would be more. The next one, the one closest to her, was already making his jumps through time. She had met him in her time and in his. He was her great grandson, King Henry II of Scotland. She had promised him the journals. She picked up her quill, dipped it in ink and started to write:

30th March 1649 – Dead. They are all dead. Grandmother and her lady's maids, Jamie, my brother King James I of England, even my husband Thomas. All dead. Now my nephew, King Charles I of England has been executed. The world has gone mad. But I have kept my purpose to the end. Now it is my turn to pass on the torch, to my son, Prince James, to be King James VII of Scotland. I have raised him well, as my grandmother raised me. He will be a great king and Scotland will prosper under his rule.

Over the years I have made a few jumps to the future to see if my purpose has played out. It has. Scotland has maintained its independence. My work is done. My days of time travel have come to an end. I will see no more lovely mornings like the one I am enjoying now, looking out my window from my private chambers at Holyrood. This was once my mother's favourite royal residence and it is my favourite too. My job is now complete. My life no longer matters, as it now sits in the pages of history. What matters now rests on the shoulders of my son and grandson, and all the Scottish royals who will follow. To maintain Scotland's independence as a strong and free country, for now and forever.'

She sighed deeply as she sat back in her chair letting her hand rest briefly. She dipped the quill again and continued her story. She wrote about growing up in Dublin, her first big jump through time at Kinross in 2018, the one that she witnessed her own birth and meeting her mother, Mary Queen of Scots. She remembered her loves, all gone now. A lifetime of memories.

She wrote about the battle at Hadrian's Wall, the battle that led to Jamie's death and about allowing her brother return to his throne in London. And she wrote about Thomas, the man she finally married, the man who fathered her children, the man who stayed by her side until his death. He never did question her decision once about crowning him king. He was happy being the Prince Consort. He earned the Scottish people's love and respect even though he hadn't been born Scottish, being the first born of the Earl of Northumberland, but when Hadrian's Wall became Scotland's new border with England, the people of Northumberland embraced Scotland as their own.

Mary Elizabeth placed the quill beside the journal and closed it. She had been writing for hours and her eyes were sore and her back ached. She was eighty years old and was now feeling every year of it. Leaning back, she let her eyelids close. Time for a breather. She didn't know how long she sat there, maybe she dozed off. Memories started flooding her mind and she realised with a jolt that she had forgotten to write everything down. She decided to make a list of dates when she had jumped, into the past and the future, and document each event.

My time is running short and there is so much more to write about. I have stayed the course and kept my purpose clear all through the years as Queen of Scotland. I developed some revolutionary ideas during my time here. Because I missed the conveniences of indoor plumbing, I took a page from Roman history and had my castles modernised, without altering the timeline that led to indoor plumbing in the future.

I was also particular about cleanliness and the proper preparation of food. The Scottish clans took note of all that I did and made similar changes to their homes.

I have always had a fondness for the arts, so I continued with what my brother had started before he left to claim the English throne. I made Edinburgh into an arts and cultural centre. I invited some of the greatest creative minds from across Europe to stay here at my court. Scientists like Isaac Newton, the English mathematician, astronomer and physicist, joined the Scottish court and helped me develop the University of Edinburgh, which had been found in 1582 during my brother's reign.

All these things cost money and lots of it. I did not raise taxes. How did I pay for it? Well, I finally managed to find my inheritance that my father had hidden. And it was a big inheritance. I myself did not need much. I was not an extravagant queen. I was not interested in lavish gowns or jewels. I lived simply and worked for my people, the Scottish people. After all, that had been my plan from the beginning, from the moment I learned that I was the daughter of Mary, Queen of Scots.

'Grandmother.'

The voice startled the queen, causing her to drop her quill.

She had lost track of time. How many days had she been working on her journals? She knew her time was near. Her loved ones were starting to appear.

'Henry,' she grasped. It was her great grandson. He was her legacy in the time travel adventure. She knew he would come, and that he would stay with her in her final hours.

'Grandmother, you are wearing yourself out.'

Mary Elizabeth smiled at the attentive young man, who would one day become King Henry of Scotland. He looked so much like the Stuarts through the generations.

'I am just about finished, and I will place all these journals in the secret compartment behind the stone over there.' She pointed to behind the hearth. She wrote in silence for a few more minutes; one of her mother's prayers. She had to include her mother at the end, as she had included her throughout the journal, and this poem was quite fitting for the closing thought of her journal.

A Prayer, written by Mary Queen of Scots, My Mother

Keep us, oh God from pettiness

Let us be large in thought, in word, in deed

Let us be done with fault-finding and leave off self-seeking

May we put away all pre-tense and meet each other

Face-to-Face with self-pity and without prejudice

May we never be hasty in judgement and be always generous

Let us take time for all things

Oh Lord, let us not forget to be kind.

Mary Elizabeth sat back to reflect on what her mother had written all those years ago. It would not be long now, and she would get to see her again. She dipped her quill in the ink one last time and wrote her final words:

Now and Forever

She stood up slowly and picked up the journal. She placed it with her grandmother's and the others and moved towards the loose stone. Pulling it out, she placed the journals carefully inside the hidden space and then replaced the stone.

'My mother's box of treasures and letters are also in there,' she said as she moved back to her seat beside the fire. Henry watched his grandmother. 'I know. I have found them in the future, just as you said I would. I have come to see you off, as you predicted I would. Are the others here yet?'

'No, but they will be soon.' He was referring to her Grandmother, Marie de Guise, Lady Mary Catherine and Jamie, of course. She waved to a chair. 'Come sit with me while I wait for them. I have so much to tell you but some I will tell you in the future. I have often wondered about the many 'what ifs. What if my grandmother had not rescued me from Loch Leven the day I was born? What if I had failed in my many attempts to claim this kingdom?'

Henry reached across to hold her hand. 'You are cold, grandmother. I should fetch you a blanket.' But Mary Elizabeth held onto his hand firmly motioning him to stay where he was.

She removed the ring that her grandmother had given to her. It had once been her grandmother's, then her mother's and finally hers. It was time to pass it on. She gazed fondly at the Stuart crest on top of the ring and handed it to Henry. 'Wear it well and keep it with you always.'

'I will grandmother,' Henry placed the ring on his baby finger. 'I am honoured.'

She then reached to her shoulder and unfastened the Stuart brooch that she had worn everyday since the first night in the cottage near Kinross. She held it in front of her noticing the fine details through her tears. She was finding it increasingly difficult to stay awake. She was fading away. Her time was near. The voice of her grandson became distant. Mary Elizabeth could no longer understand what he was saying.

Looking beyond Henry, her faced brightened and she beamed the brightest smile. Henry looked up and noticed his grandmother's smile, her look of pure joy as her eyes locked with someone standing behind him. Fastening the brooch to his tunic, he followed her gaze.

'You have come, Grandmother, Lady Mary Catherine, Jamie,' she said. 'And just in time.' Shadows of figures moved by the window, taking shape, there were three. They each nodded at Henry, then beckoned to Mary Elizabeth. When Henry looked back at his grandmother she was slumped over her chair. He felt for her pulse. There was none.

'Now and forever, grandmother,' he said as his tears ran down his cheeks. 'I will see you in the future.

Now and forever

ABOUT THE AUTHOR

Suzanne Maria Byrne is the author of several books, including The Kings & Queens of the Tudor & Stuart Dynasties, Grace O'Malley Ireland's Pirate Queen and more recently My Highland Laird, her first Scottish historical romance novel.

She writes about historical figures, mainly in the 16th and 17th centuries. Her real passion is the history of Scotland especially her studies on Mary, Queen of Scots, who she is obsessed with.

She is the creator of The History Writer Files website. A reference site containing information on the people and places of the 15th, 16th & 17th centuries.

She lives in Dublin, Ireland with her husband and daughter.

20105540R00086

Printed in Great Britain
by Amazon